LIVING AMONG US

DEBBIE KUMP

World Castle Publishing, LLC
Pensacola, Florida
Copyright © Debbie Kump 2021
Paperback ISBN: 9781955086820
eBook ISBN: 9781955086837
First Edition World Castle Publishing, LLC, September 13, 2021
http://www.worldcastlepublishing.com

Licensing Notes

Cover: Karen Fuller
Editor: Maxine Bringenberg

DEDICATION

For Apollo

PROLOGUE

Casey Donnelly couldn't have asked for a better day. After spending the past week cooped up in his cousin's house with his mom and extended family, the storm had finally headed away from the Carolina coast, leaving a trail of crystal clear skies and perfect swells in its wake.

Finally, this vacation can begin, Casey thought as Aunt Samantha and Uncle Jim unpacked boogie boards, beach towels, a picnic lunch, and the umbrella from their minivan. Arms loaded with gear, he followed them a great distance across the crowded parking lot and over the dunes. A flock of noisy gulls soared overhead, greeting their arrival.

Casey's anticipation mounted when he saw the waves crash onto the beach, and the aroma of caramel popcorn with a dash of sea salt filled his nose. Once they found a suitable spot to set up their towels and chairs away from the surf, his cousin, Jason, dropped his contents in the sand in exchange for a bright yellow boogie board. "Let's go, Casey!" he called, and excitedly darted toward the water's edge. Jason's sandy blond hair bounced with each stride.

Casey cast an expectant glance at his mom, wondering if she'd make him finish setting up the chairs and umbrellas before he could join Jason in the surf.

Before she could reply, Uncle Jim offered, "It's okay, Ellen. Casey can go. I've got it from here." He handed Casey a blue and white striped boogie board from the pile.

"Thanks!" Casey smiled and turned on his heels toward the water, the summer sun beating upon his back. He fumbled to secure the Velcro on the wrist leash as he ran, trying to catch his older cousin. Having a two-year advantage, Jason was always faster and stronger at everything, no matter how hard Casey tried to keep up with him.

Casey sprinted to the water's edge, leaving a trail of footprints in the hard, wet sand. Before entering the water, he paused for a moment to survey the scene. A dark swell rose with impressive power, toppling into a foamy surge that scooped up the boogie boarders and quickly deposited them on the sloped beach. Casey's blue eyes brightened. He tucked the board under his arm and charged toward the sea, splashing through the shallows to join Jason. An incoming wave collided with him, forcing Casey a step backward. He stumbled briefly, then pressed onward. Flopping onto his board, he coasted over the top of the next approaching wave and zoomed down its backside.

"Glad you finally made it," Jason said with mock congratulations.

Casey rolled his eyes. One of these days, he would find something he could do better and faster than Jason.

"Look…a good one's coming," Jason announced, and turned his board toward shore to prepare for the ride.

"Really?" Casey asked, secretly wishing he had spent more time at the ocean so he could make predictions like Jason. He looked out to sea, where a deep blue mass loomed, rising much higher than its predecessors.

"Whoa." Jason let out a low whistle. "Get ready," he

advised.

Casey mimicked Jason's actions, facing the tip of his boogie board toward the beach so the wave could sweep him up with its growing power. With his board set in a ready position, Casey kicked his feet madly, trying to catch the rising swell. A wall of water towered above him, outlined in white surging foam against the crisp cerulean sky. Casey watched expectantly. The crest curled over the top of his head, then unleashed its fury upon him.

Casey closed his eyes and held his breath a second before the forceful wave dragged him under. The power of the water rolled him like an amusement park ride. The tumbling water should have confused his every sense of direction, but Casey felt perfectly at ease in its grasp. Churning bubbles swirled and brushed his face. Sand suspended in the water mingled with his hair. His knees struck the sandy bottom and reoriented him. He planted his feet and gave a swift kick to resurface. He instantly located his bobbing board and threw one arm across it for support.

A wide grin filled Casey's face. He shook the water from his floppy auburn hair and mopped the seawater from his eyes. Turning to his cousin, he exclaimed, "That was awesome!"

Only Jason was no longer there.

That wave was huge...how was Jason able to actually ride it all the way into shore? Casey laughed in wonder, awestruck at his cousin's superior skill in every facet of their lives. He looked toward the beach, expecting to see Jason dragging himself from the water to prepare for another ride. Yet, he couldn't spot Jason anywhere. It didn't make any sense; his cousin had been right beside him before that wave broke over his head. How could he lose sight of Jason that quickly?

Casey wheeled his head around, his grin quickly fading. With each passing second, fear replaced his initial elation. He scanned the sea in all directions for a sign of Jason. To his left, kids played tag, teens threw a football in the shallow water, and others body surfed or boogie boarded the next set of swells. Yet on his right, he saw a small area where the waves didn't break. This water appeared curiously free of beachgoers. When he followed that smooth patch of water, he noticed a small, bright yellow object far out at sea. He squinted into the distance, not believing his eyes. Clinging to the yellow board, a figure frantically waved one arm over his head, his wet hair plastered against his forehead.

Jason.

Casey glanced back at the lifeguard stand, hoping someone else had noticed Jason's cry for help. Casey expected to find an attentive lifeguard clad in a white tank top with a red cross emblazoned on its front, diligently poised on the edge of his chair. Only the chair sat empty. Casey vaguely recalled passing a sign that read *NO LIFEGUARD ON DUTY* when he had tried to fasten the board's leash to his wrist in his eager dash to the water. His eyes flickered toward Aunt Samantha's colorful beach umbrella where his family relaxed in the shade, absorbed with their tablets and phones…completely unaware of Jason's plight. He didn't have time to alert them. Every precious second wasted could spell disaster.

Casey needed to act fast before the current dragged Jason farther out to sea. He blinked to focus. When he reopened his eyes, the brilliant blue-green color of the water had changed. The nearby strip of water that remained peculiarly free of waves now flashed crimson in warning: the color of death. Casey's jaw dropped in horror, watching the water rush away from shore in a swift current. How hadn't he noticed it before?

Without wasting time to ponder the inexplicable color change, Casey turned his board to intercept the current and kicked furiously to catch up to Jason. The water of the crimson current moved at a much faster rate, opposite the rush of the waves toward the shoreline. With minimal effort, Casey quickly spanned the distance between them.

As he neared, Casey saw his cousin's face bleached with

panic. With one arm clinging desperately to his board, Jason frenetically flailed his free hand to signal for help. Another wave grew behind him, its white crest curling as it lifted Jason up in its surging power. It dropped him in its wake, dousing his head with frothy seawater before its energy reached Casey. He rode the same swell upward, losing sight of Jason for a moment behind the mass of water. Once the wave had passed and the ocean flattened, Casey saw the yellow board bobbing alone on the surface.

Thinking fast, Casey slipped the Velcro from his wrist, freeing himself from the buoyant board and its leash. He knew he'd need the board for flotation back to shore, but first, he must find Jason. Casey ducked underwater and opened his eyes. A flurry of bubbles dissolved around him, allowing him to see more clearly into the crimson water, surprisingly translucent in nature. He spun his head from one side to the other, searching for a sign against the uniform background. In an instant, he spotted Jason's dark form sinking helplessly downward. He had to act quickly; every second mattered. With swift strokes, Casey dove after him. His legs kicked like a pair of scissors slicing through the water, his cupped hands forcing him further with each pull. He thought nothing of his finite air supply as he pushed his body to move faster through the water in a frantic race against time.

Finally reaching him, Casey slipped one arm across Jason's chest and locked his hand under his cousin's armpit. With a secure grasp, Casey kicked madly, pulling huge handfuls of the reddish water with his cousin in tow. He looked up, ignoring the great distance that remained between them and the bright sky far above. Sunlight filtered through the water column in bright, welcoming bands, just out of reach.

He kept his gaze focused on the pale yellow light cutting through the blood red water. Casey forced himself to ignore the burn growing within his chest. His body begged for relief as the volume of air that filled his lungs grew disparagingly thin.

We will make it back, he promised himself. The desperate stab at confidence strengthened his will in the struggle to the surface.

Moments later, Casey broke through, greeting the air with eager breaths. He gasped, his throat scratchy and harsh from the exertion of his ascent. He wanted to exclaim to Jason, "We did it!" but the words couldn't come out. All of his effort was now devoted to supporting Jason's head above the surf, kicking his legs robotically to tread water for the both of them. One wave after another washed over them, lifting then dropping the floating boys like a roller coaster over a series of hills in the track. Casey's heart lightened when he heard Jason cough to expel the seawater from his lungs.

"Now, let's get you back to shore."

Keeping one arm wrapped around Jason, Casey spun his head, grateful to rest on their boogie boards on the way back.

Except the boards had vanished.

The current must have carried them away, Casey thought. A new wave of horror consumed his thoughts. The shoreline looked so far away. How could he possibly make it back to safety without the boards? He had counted on them to help carry Jason since he definitely couldn't swim on his own. There must be something he could use, but when he cast a quick glance in each direction, he saw only water, one wave after another.

Casey took a deep breath, steeling his resolve. He had no other choice. He must finish this on his own.

Swimming parallel to shore to avoid the rush of the rip current's crimson water flowing far out into the Atlantic, Casey began the long journey back, pushing all thoughts of fatigue to the recesses of his mind. No one had seen them dragged away. No lifeguard would come to their aid. He had to finish this alone or accept a finality he refused to recognize. Dismissing that terrible thought, he kept swimming. Each successive stroke and kick of his legs came with grueling effort.

"Almost there," he reassured Jason every few strokes,

hoping the surety in his voice would buoy his own confidence. Struggling to keep Jason's head above water, he battled the surf, forever keeping his gaze glued to the beach. He fought the growing burn in his arms and cramping in his calves. He choked on the briny water when the wave caps crashed against his face. Salt stung at his eyes, but still, he pressed on, grateful to feel the steady rise and fall of Jason's chest against his arm. His cousin hadn't managed to speak, but at least he was breathing and conscious. Casey prayed that was enough for now.

One long minute strung into the next as he battled the waves for the better part of a half hour. Soon the shore graciously drew near. On the shoreline, he spotted Aunt Samantha and his mom expectantly watching their return. Even from this distance, Casey could see their faces creased with dread.

Uncle Jim pointed, shouting, "There they are!" Concerned bystanders turned their heads as Casey's mom, aunt, and uncle dashed into the water.

Casey's strength renewed with joy. With sudden vigor, he swam harder, anxious to intercept them. Just as the sand brushed the bottom of his feet, his family reached them.

"Thank God you're safe." Uncle Jim threw his arms around the boys with relief, then lifted Jason from Casey's grasp.

Casey's tired arms fell limp against his sides. His legs crumbled beneath him, overcome with exhaustion. Aunt Samantha swept his arm over her shoulders, helping him regain his footing. "Thank you. Oh, thank you," she wept, planting a grateful kiss on each of Casey's cheeks.

"I'm so happy to know you're okay," Ellen cried. She swept him into a tight embrace and helped Aunt Samantha carry him the last few feet, setting him safely on the sand beyond the water's reach.

A crowd quickly gathered around them, uttering hushed whispers of concern. Wide-eyed children clung tightly to their parents' hands as they watched with curiosity. Some voices carried above the others as more beachgoers drew near, leaving the water and their blankets and umbrellas behind.

"That's a strong rip current," one elderly woman in a broad sunhat warned. "They're very dangerous. You're lucky to be alive."

"He's a hero!" a young boy wearing arm floaties and a baseball cap exclaimed, bobbing up and down on his heels with excitement.

"How old are you, son?" asked a middle-aged man, his tanned skin weathered from years spent shirtless beneath the southern sun.

"He's only ten," Ellen answered for him. He noticed her voice still shook as she spoke.

"Only ten. That's remarkable," the man added, nodding in an impressed way. "Well, I guess with your talent in swimming, we should be expecting to see you in the Olympics someday." He gave Casey a big thumbs-up.

Hero? Olympics? Casey's eyes grew wide, and his heart swelled with pride. Jason had always been better than him at everything, but this time Casey had proven himself; the one time when it really mattered. Casey couldn't imagine what terrible fate might have occurred if he hadn't acted immediately. Instinct had kicked in; anyone else would've done the same. Except something in the back of his head told him the man was right. He shouldn't have been able to escape a rip current with his cousin in tow. Not at his young age.

Casey turned his head toward his cousin. Jason's wet hair was plastered against his cheeks, hiding most of his face from view. Aunt Samantha and Uncle Jim knelt nearby, patting Jason's back as he coughed up seawater. Casey ignored the crowd's comments as he looked on with worry. Finally, Jason finished coughing. He took a few deep breaths, settling his emotions from the ordeal, then flashed Casey a broad, appreciative smile.

Casey heaved a sigh of relief. Jason would be okay. And

Casey had learned something about himself in the process. Maybe he was a better swimmer than he'd ever imagined.

His mom sighed deeply as if driving terrible thoughts from her mind. She swept his matted hair off his forehead and placed her palms against his cheeks. "You are so brave. I don't know how you managed to save Jason and yourself."

As the crowd began to thin, Casey told her how the current looked a deep red, and he followed the colored path out to Jason. He explained how the waves had dragged Jason under, but he spotted his cousin's silhouetted body against the background of reddish water. He grabbed Jason and brought him back to the surface, only to realize that their boards had drifted away. The only choice he had was to swim back to shore.

Ellen brushed her windswept hair from her face and glanced out to sea. When she turned back to Casey, her pale green eyes surveyed him with a mix of confusion and alarm. "Are you sure? I don't see any red water. It all looks blue to me."

Casey blinked. To him, the rip current remained a distinct crimson path, easy to recognize against the blue-green seawater, warning others of its danger. How couldn't she notice it?

He opened his mouth to protest, then reconsidered. The concern inscribed upon his mom's face cautioned him from saying more. Casey knew in that instant, something about him was different. He had no idea how different, but he was determined to find out.

CHAPTER ONE

Carrying his goggles and swim cap, Casey set his gaze on the framed team records set in changeable type on a track board hanging high on the wall. He stretched out his arms on his way to the starting blocks, repeating the lowest recorded time for this event in his mind. It wasn't enough to simply beat Westlake High School's pool record—he intended to destroy it.

Once he reached lane three, he dipped his gold cap into the water to fill it to the brim, then dumped it over his thick auburn hair, tucking every strand in place underneath his school's navy blue "W" printed on each side. He shook out his arms and jumped up and down exactly three times to loosen his leg muscles. This ritual helped focus Casey's attention and revitalize his senses. Years ago, he'd discovered the cool water made his senses surprisingly alert, battling the calming effects of the pool area's warm, humid air. Laced with the scent of chlorine and a faint hint of homemade chocolate chip cookies, the smell of the pool made Casey feel right at home. He let the beads of water run down his arms and bare chest, focusing his efforts on the number fixed in his mind.

He glanced at the competition to his right, then to his left, knowing he would be racing himself more than the other swimmers in this two hundred yard individual medley in order to achieve his goal. He adjusted his goggles strap in just the right place over his cap and told himself, "I can do this." He shook his head, displeased with his lack of conviction. Amending his original comment, he steeled his mind with resolution. "I *will* do this...today."

"Swimmers, take your marks," the race announcer declared.

Casey bent over to grasp the starting block, his muscles tight and ready to spring. He lifted his head, his attention trained on the other side of the pool twenty-five yards away and how little time he needed to span that entire distance. Two lengths of butterfly, followed by two lengths of backstroke, made up the first half of the race. He'd then double that distance with two lengths of breaststroke and finally two lengths of freestyle.

Easy. He'd trained for this. He could do this; the record would soon be his to claim. He waited for the start with one hundred percent of his focus. Ready to spring into action.

BEEEEEEP. The horn blared, and six swimmers instantly exploded off the starting blocks in unison.

Casey rocketed through the air, his body piking at the waist in the middle of his dive. He tucked one hand over the other, his arms pressed tightly against his ears, creating the smallest possible opening for his body to transition from the air into the liquid realm. From his years of training, Casey knew streamlining his body to reduce drag provided the best opportunity to cement his lead in the first leg of this race.

He entered the pool with minimal splash. The cool water ran across his skin with enhanced perceptions, like every exposed nerve ending tingled with heightened alertness. Instantly, his view of the water transformed from the monochromatic blue others observed to a palette of informative colors. Even though he wore clear goggles, a flurry of pale yellow and mint green bubbles filled his vision. He noticed every eddy off the other swimmers or reflected waves off the lane lines as a red-tinged warning, similar to the crimson rip current along the Carolina coast that had nearly dragged his cousin to his death six and a half years ago. Rescuing Jason marked the first time Casey could read the water…and he'd become much more attuned to its nuances ever since.

The path of least resistance appeared in swirling shades of teal green and aquamarine blue, like a traffic light signaling his ideal opportunity to proceed. With each efficient stroke, Casey used the revealing colors of the water to optimize his performance and seal his success in this race. But he never told anyone about the colors he saw in the water, not after his mom's reaction all those years ago at the beach. Instead, he attributed his success on other measurable factors: years of effort, dedication, and sacrifice.

His feet locked together in a butterfly kick, undulating up and down in synchrony like the powerful tail fluke of a dolphin. Maintaining his streamlined form, he surged forward underwater. Over halfway down the length of the pool, he surfaced. His sweeping arms broke through the water in synchronized arcs. Several strong butterfly strokes later, he reached the wall. Already, Casey commanded a sizeable lead on his competition.

Go faster, Casey urged himself, propelling his body out of the turn with considerable force. Though his muscles burned from exertion, his stroke appeared effortless to those watching from the stands. He heard their muffled cheers each time his face left the water for a brief breath.

Casey zoomed out of his next turn and transitioned into the backstroke. With his face above water for this second section of the race, he lacked the ability to differentiate between the bold, bright colors of the water and the path of least resistance until his flip turns. Instead, he relied on the tactile sensation of grasping long pulls of new, smooth water to further his lead. Casey normally enjoyed the diversity of this event, completing two lengths of the four strokes. But today, his brain switched into automaton mode, focusing strictly on his practiced mechanics to increase the effectiveness of each pull and kick.

Starting on the third leg of his race, Casey's head bobbed out of the water on each breaststroke pull. He noticed his competition lagged farther behind on every turn. Yet, he didn't relent. Instead, he kept pushing himself to swim faster and harder, widening the gap between him and the others while the colors of the water directed his route. In no time, he had finished two lengths of breaststroke and began his rapid freestyle.

Even though Casey had reached the final leg of this race, he had trained himself to limit his gulps of air during races. The mere action of turning his head to the side for a breath created unnecessary drag and could slow his speed by a few hundredths of a second. He feared those few precious hundredths might cost him the record. Typically, he allowed himself two or three breaths per length of freestyle. This time, he reduced that number to one.

Despite his tremendous effort, Casey's body felt naturally relaxed in the water. The pool infused him with unusual strength, a sensation he felt nowhere else. He practiced long hours every day, shaping his muscles for the essential speed to carry him through his sprints. Now he honed his entire focus on reaching the distant wall in the shortest amount of time. With deep, efficient pulls and strong, swift kicks, he raced the final yards at an unprecedented pace. Finally nearing the end, he turned his head to extend his reach and drove his hand hard into the wall, signaling the stop pad to record his time.

He hoped he had swum fast enough, though only the numbers on the stop pad's timer would say for sure. The advantageous colors faded from view when Casey lifted his head out of the water. His chest heaved with exertion. This time, he permitted his lungs to take in their fill. Removing his goggles and cap off his head, he shook the water from his hair. He habitually looked toward his coach for approval and then his mother in the stands. As a social studies teacher at the neighboring middle school, she had nearly the same schedule as Casey and never missed one of his races.

Before he could spot either, a radiant face greeted him with a dazzling smile. Her bright yellow top stood out against her deep skin tones and the uniform tiles lining the walls, reminding him of the color of daffodils in the spring. "Congratulations, Casey!" she exclaimed and squatted down in her fitted and fashionably torn jeans by the end of his lane. She stuck out a hand to shake his. "My name's Mandi Howe. Can I get your picture for the school newspaper?"

"You're in my biology class," Casey casually noted.

Although she replied, "Oh, right!" the look on her face belied her sentiment into something more like, "Really?" which didn't entirely surprise Casey. Her popular circle rarely overlapped with his friend group.

"Anyway," Mandi quickly recovered, casually tucking a lock of her long, curly hair behind her ear to mask her discomfort. "How about that picture?"

Casey blinked. As much as he yearned to know his time, Mandi's bouncy brown hair and bright chocolate eyes captivated him. He figured he must have done pretty well if Mandi Howe wanted his photo for the Westlake student news. "Sure," he said, running his fingers through his mop of wet hair in a poor attempt of taming it. He gave her a wide grin.

Mandi straightened and slipped her phone from her back pocket. She slid her fingers across the screen to crop his image just how she wanted, then aimed at Casey. Her lips drew into a natural smile as if she were the subject of the photograph. She tapped her finger against the screen and said, "Smile!" The camera's flash blinded him, making stars cloud his vision, but she didn't seem to notice. "I'm writing a piece on stand-out athletes," she explained. "Do you think I could interview you after the meet?"

Her genuine interest in his performance surprised him, especially since she hadn't seemed to notice him all year in biology. Still, her startling appearance dulled his senses, just like every time he saw her on the daily televised school news broadcasts, in class, or featured in the school paper.

He shrugged his shoulders and gave a delayed response. "Sure," he said, immediately kicking himself for using the same dull, monosyllabic reply. He'd better figure out a way to keep his mind focused on providing more insightful responses during the interview, or her interest in him would fade faster than any record he'd potentially broken.

Mandi nodded politely. "Thanks," she replied, then turned on her heels.

"Wait, how'd I do?" Casey asked before she could leave.

She stopped, spinning back around to face him. She gave him an approving thumbs-up.

Ignoring the lingering fatigue in his arms and legs, he pulled himself out of the pool in a single fluid motion, eager to hear the results. Water poured off his body and splashed into the deck's drain. He felt bad for getting her tennis shoes and the bottom of her jeans a little wet, but she didn't seem to care.

Her eyebrows raised with excitement. "You shattered the pool record by 3.4 seconds," she announced in an impressed tone.

Casey pumped his fist with elation. *Three point four seconds under!* His heart swelled with pride.

"Well, I guess I'll see you after the meet," Mandi said. With a wink, she turned on her heels and rejoined the fans in the stands, catching herself as she slipped slightly on the wet pool deck.

Casey watched her leave, wondering if her wink suggested anything beyond the article for the school newspaper.

* * * *

"I'm so proud of you, Casey," Ellen Donnelly gushed after the meet, finding him the second he left the locker room with his backpack from school and duffel bag of wet swim gear. She wrapped her arms around him in a tight hug that would normally make him feel uncomfortable in public. But after all she'd done to help support his swimming career over the years, he owed it to her to let her feel proud of his accomplishment tonight. He let his duffel bag slide off his shoulder and drop to the ground to return her embrace. Three point four seconds under! Casey congratulated himself by letting the number dance through his mind for a long moment.

His mom released him from her arms. "So, what would you like to do to celebrate?" He noticed a trace of joyful tears welling up in her pale green eyes. Usually, they'd order a pizza or go out for a bite to eat after he'd had a great race.

"Um," he replied, noncommittal. His eyes shifted down the hall, where he spotted Mandi Howe leaning against the wall. She'd thrown a heather gray hoodie over her bright yellow short-sleeved shirt since he last saw her inside the warmth of the pool area, but wet rings still circled the bottoms of her jeans from when he had exited the water. He frowned at his thoughtlessness, especially when the outside temperature regularly dipped below zero at this time of year in Minnesota. She twirled a lock of her curly brown hair between her fingers as if lost in thought, then let it drop so she could jot a few notes onto her tablet. Perhaps questions for the interview, Casey guessed.

"Can I meet you back at home?" he asked his mom, bending down to pick up his duffle bag. He threw it back over his shoulder. "Someone from the school paper asked to interview me." He glanced in Mandi's direction, trying to keep his face expressionless. It would be way too embarrassing to start blushing in front of his mom.

Ellen followed his gaze. "Not a problem," she replied. "I, um, guess I'll leave a plate for you to reheat instead. How's that sound?"

He nodded, only catching half of her reply.

She placed her hand on his shoulder and gave a small squeeze. "Good luck!"

With his mother headed toward the parking lot, Casey walked in the opposite direction down the hall, running through a list of possible questions Mandi might ask and what he could say that would sound decently intelligent and not overly contrived in return. Keep it simple, he reminded himself, and don't disclose too much. Yet all of his preparation fled his mind the instant he opened his mouth to address her.

"Hey," Casey said simply. He pointed at her feet and uttered the first thought that entered his mind. "Sorry about your jeans."

Mandi looked up from her work. "Huh?"

Casey swallowed. "I didn't mean to get you wet when I got out of the pool." He frowned. That hadn't come out like he'd planned.

She gave a small laugh. "No, you're good. Anything for a story, right? Besides, it'll teach me to roll them up to my knees next time." She nervously tucked a curl of hair behind her ear. "So, um, I've prepared a bunch of questions to ask, if that's okay with you." She shifted her tablet to one hand and pulled her phone out of her back pocket. "Do you mind if I video the interview? I'm not the fastest writer, and I don't want to miss anything."

"That's fine," Casey agreed. He set his backpack and duffel bag out of the way. He ran his fingers through his damp auburn hair a few times to settle it down, then squared his shoulders before she began, hoping to release some of the apprehension of sounding like an idiot in front of all of Westlake High.

"Okay," she said, and pressed the record button on her phone. "First question: how did you feel when you broke the pool record today?"

Phew. At least she started with an easy one, he thought, letting the tension in his shoulders subside a bit. He took a deep breath, then gave a proud smile. "Pretty amazing." He had worked so hard for so many years to reach this level of competition. Breaking school records and pool records would definitely help in gaining recognition from college scouts in the area. "I've been training for that event for the past few years, so I was pretty ready for it."

Casey winced at his choice of words. He had just uttered the word "pretty" twice in two consecutive sentences. Mandi didn't have to be a genius to read his thoughts. Time to try a different tactic, he scolded himself. Maybe he'd have better luck with composing more introspective responses if he didn't look straight at her when answering.

Fortunately, she didn't seem to notice. "And when did you first begin swimming?" she continued.

"I joined the swim team when I was ten."

Casey thought back to the circumstances that led to that decision, grateful for a distraction from his thoughts. After listening to the crowd's comments that day at the beach, Casey couldn't get the idea of swimming competitively out of his mind. For weeks, he begged his mom to let him join the local club team until she eventually relented. He had finally found his niche, something he excelled in. Something he could do better than his cousin, Jason.

"What made you choose swimming?" she asked, following up on his reply.

He shrugged, selecting a casual answer rather than going into the details of that nearly tragic day. "Swimming is natural for me. I guess you could say I can 'read' the water," he replied, realizing only too late that he should have omitted this detail as well.

"'Read' the water?" Mandi's thin eyebrows twisted with intrigue. She studied him with her deep brown eyes, puzzled by his unexpected response. "What do you mean by that? Like you can read the water like you can read words in a book?"

Casey regretted bringing this up. What happened to his plan of keeping this interview simple and not going into too much detail? If she used her video on the daily news broadcast, the whole school would know his secret. Then again, she had said it was for an article in the school newspaper. Not that many people actually read the school paper, right? "Not exactly," he said, trying to make his ability sound completely normal. "It's more like I can feel the currents off my fingertips and see the path of least resistance."

"I've never heard of that before." Mandi scratched her head in confusion. "Have you always been able to do that?"

"Not that I know of. I first noticed it on a trip to visit my cousin in North Carolina." He immediately kicked himself for bringing this up.

"How's that?" she prompted, eager for more.

Frustrated with himself, Casey quickly summed up how a casual day of boogie boarding turned into a near disaster when the rip current had swept his cousin out to sea.

"You're kidding." Mandi's mouth fell open. For a moment, she stared at him without blinking. She shook her head as if to refocus. "This keeps getting better and better. Go on," she prodded, eager to hear more. She raised her cell phone closer to Casey to guarantee she didn't miss a word.

He certainly hadn't meant to paint himself like a hero, but the story naturally lent itself that way, he supposed. So Casey went on to explain how he received such a warm welcome when he returned to shore that he couldn't imagine pursuing any other sport. However, he made sure to omit the part of the rip current's red color of warning that streaked the blue ocean water and the spectrum of colors he noticed in what others perceived as a monochromatic pool. Even if only one person actually read her article, rumors would spread like wildfire through the school and social media. He didn't need the entire student body thinking he was nuts.

Mandi appeared spellbound with his words, listening with rapt attention, to the point he noticed she hadn't blinked once during his entire story. He reminded himself to stop looking at her and focus on his responses in simple yet coherent sentences.

Casey stopped talking at the end of his story, but his mind continued rolling through memories of the events that followed Jason's rescue. Shortly after they returned home from North Carolina that summer, his mom brought him to the doctor for an eye exam. Perhaps he possessed some type of visual impairment or color blindness that accounted for his vision of the reddish current, his mom reasoned. Instead, the doctor diagnosed him with synesthesia.

Casey once read that the term *synesthesia* originated from two Greek words: *syn* meaning "together" and *aesthesis* meaning "perception," like his perceptions or senses of the world coexisted in a joined or fused state. His doctor often described his condition as a fusion of multiple senses.

Casey wasn't convinced this perfectly explained his ability to read the water, but so far, nothing else had come closer. He did exhibit some of the traits of synesthesia, like favoring his left hand and having some related words associated with particular colors of the spectrum. For instance, the word "water" always took on a turquoise color in his mind, whereas "ocean" was seafoam green and "pool" was sapphire blue. "Lake" looked a light shade of violet, and "sea" a deep pink, close to fuchsia.

But Casey noticed these colors only appeared in water-related terms, unlike other people with synesthesia who viewed a rainbow of colors or perceived a bouquet of aromas in the black and white print of a textbook. For them, each individual letter often matched consistently with a specific color or a particular scent. Others diagnosed with synesthesia associated senses with types of instruments, like a French horn might sound orange or a tuba's blast might trigger the taste of blueberries. For some, a flute's melody felt like a soft breeze against their cheeks, or the number twenty-four smelled like vanilla. Still others could recognize specific shapes through distinct tastes in their mouths.

Casey was quick to mention to his doctor that he didn't possess any of these other symptoms, but the doctor assured him that every case of synesthesia was unique since different parts of the brain became intricately cross-wired. Not all people with this condition viewed letters, numbers, sounds, or feelings the same way. So Casey accepted the medical explanation and moved on, focusing his efforts on his sport instead, and learning how to read the water to his advantage.

Mandi's voice snapped him from his thoughts, and for a quick second, he commended himself for keeping that last bit of information private. He really didn't think she, or anyone for that matter, would understand the scents and colors he associated with words. He blinked at Mandi, who seemed to be waiting for his reply. "I'm sorry?" he said, realizing he had missed her question altogether.

She nodded, then started again. "You made an amazing accomplishment today. That pool record has stood for nearly a decade. Your mom and dad must be very proud."

Casey smiled uncomfortably. "My mom is. But my father…." His voice trailed off, his smile rapidly fading as if her topic had entered dark and dangerous water.

"My bad," Mandi said, guilt rising in her chocolate eyes. "I didn't mean—"

"No, it's okay. It's not your fault." His eyes found his feet. Casey didn't know how to explain. How could he, when he knew so little about the man who had left them soon after he was born?

Mandi gracefully changed the subject. "Okay, so I've got one last question for you: what do you see as your future plans for swimming?"

Luckily, that was an easy one for Casey to answer. He pushed conflicted thoughts about his father to the back of his mind and elaborated on the dreams he'd held since that day back on the Carolina beach. "We've got Sections in two weeks before I start tapering for States, and then…well…hopefully I'll be ready for the Olympic Trials."

Her eyes widened. "Wow," she said, her voice breathless with amazement. "Like *The* Olympics?"

He nodded. "It's been my dream since I was a little kid."

"And you think you've got a shot?" she asked, incredulous.

"Coach thinks so," he replied, trying to keep some humility in his tone after his slip with his heroic-sounding rescue.

She noted, "I saw on your schedule you've got your last home meet next week."

"Yeah. One step at a time, I guess."

"I'll be there." Mandi beamed. "I wouldn't want to miss the sequel to this story." She pressed a button on her phone to stop the recording.

Casey frowned. *The sequel to her story.* Why did he mislead himself into thinking she was the slightest bit interested in him for anything besides a news story? He was foolish to let himself grow absorbed with her dazzling appearance. Besides, he didn't have time for distractions right now, not this close to the end of the season. His last and toughest races were still to come. With a sigh, he picked up his backpack and duffel bag and turned for the door, shifting his attention instead to the plate of leftovers waiting for him at home.

"Hey, Casey, are you busy right now?" Mandi asked, and slipped her phone into the back pocket of her jeans. "Off the record, of course," she added with a soft smile that brought out the dimples in her cheeks.

He stopped in his tracks and spun to face Mandi. "No, not really. Why?"

"Well, I was wondering if you'd like to join me for coffee. Of course, you're probably on a strict diet since you're still training," she quickly added, "but I think they have fruit smoothies or chocolate milk if that would work."

Casey instantly drove his worries about unnecessary distractions to the back of his mind. Maybe she was interested in more than just her news story after all. Plus, he still had plenty of time to prepare for his next race.

He grinned. "Sure. Chocolate milk sounds great."

CHAPTER TWO

The next day in biology class, Casey suppressed a smile when Mandi Howe paused her conversation to wave to him when he walked in the room. He tried to reply with a casual wave back but doubted he successfully contained the blush from rising up into his cheeks. He took his seat and pretended to look busy fishing his notebook and pencil from his backpack; he didn't want to seem too interested.

Still, his mind drifted back to their conversation from the night before at the coffee shop, running through every word in the hopes he hadn't said anything to embarrass himself too badly. At least she was kind enough to avoid asking him any more questions about his father or reading the water. Instead, their conversation drifted toward easy, neutral topics like school and movies. He allowed himself a small breath of relief. He couldn't have messed up talking that much if she had bothered to wave to him, right?

Of course, Casey missed Mrs. Davidson's entire introduction to their new unit on ecology as his mind lingered on the night before. While his classmates had already begun to record the notes from the slides, he scrambled to locate his biology notebook and pencil somewhere in the depths of his backpack.

Finally gathering his supplies, Casey opened to a random page and started writing furiously to catch up when he caught the distinct sound of gurgling water from the drinking fountain down the hall. Suddenly, the taste of homemade apple pie topped with a big helping of whipped cream filled his mouth. His stomach gave an angry growl, reminding him that he still had another three periods before lunch. He pressed his hand against his stomach, hoping no one had heard, and swallowed hard, wishing he could wash the tempting taste down his throat. It faded as soon as the water fountain stopped, allowing Casey a moment to focus again on his notes. With dismay, he realized he had missed every word of the lecture so far. Unable to change the past, his pencil flew across the page, trying to get down all of the words before she moved on to the next slide. He was hoping it would be enough to study from when the periodic drip from one of the sinks in the back of the classroom rang through his ears. He stopped writing and swiveled his head from side to side to locate the source of the sound, which Casey found odd that no one else seemed to notice. He knew they had a huge chapter test coming up, but despite his best efforts, he found it exceedingly difficult to concentrate on the lesson.

With all of the distractions nearby, he barely caught Mrs. Davidson's instructions after notes. Casey's eyes shifted from one neighbor to the next, trying to figure out what to do. Meanwhile, the rest of the class had already whipped open the cases on their tablets. Casey craned his head across the aisle. "Psst, Rohan. Which one do I open?" he whispered and pointed to his screen, grateful his teammate sat only a desk away.

Rohan Chopra rolled his dark brown eyes, the color of coffee with just a drop of cream, and shot him a look that read, *Weren't you paying attention?* Still, he tilted his tablet so Casey could catch the title.

"Thanks," he whispered again, but Rohan had already returned his attention to the front of the class. Casey read through the directions quickly. *Pretty simple*, he thought, *just read and highlight a passage on food chains and food webs.*

He took a deep breath. No big deal. Maybe he hadn't missed that much after all.

Casey's eyes skimmed over the opening paragraphs on top predators, carnivores, herbivores, and autotrophs, describing plants and other organisms that could make their own food. When he flipped his screen to a picture of a food chain from a marine ecosystem, a flood of images filled his mind. He saw the oceanic dwellers riding a rush of scarlet water up the Carolina shoreline, each organism quickly consumed in the jaws of the successively larger creature. His skin tingled like cool coastal waters were washing across his body. He closed his eyes to refocus, then looked again. Words scattered across the document leapt out at him in bright colors of the rainbow.

He raised his hand, certain he must have missed some of her directions when his mind had taken a detour.

As soon as she finished helping one of his classmates, Mrs. Davidson gave him a quick nod and walked over to his spot. "Yes, Casey?" she asked, pushing her glasses up her thin nose.

"I'm a little confused," he admitted. "I thought you wanted us to highlight the passage."

"That's right," she agreed.

"But mine's already done," he explained, pointing to the colored words throughout the document. "Did you happen to give me the answer key by mistake?"

Mrs. Davidson glanced at his screen, then wrinkled her brow. "Casey, I'm not sure what you're talking about. Nothing on this page is highlighted yet." She repeated the directions for him before moving on to help another student, making Casey feel like he shouldn't have bothered to waste her time.

He sank low in his seat, hoping Mandi hadn't noticed him

talking to Mrs. Davidson. Obviously, the directions were simple enough to understand. What he couldn't figure out was why his screen remained illuminated in multiple colors. Things like this always seemed to happen to him, but he didn't think others, especially her, would understand. Few kids his age would bother to comprehend or accept anything that deviated that far from society's view of normal.

Completing the assignment took extraordinary focus. Casey attempted to ignore the bright colored words leaping off his screen. Instead, he tried to concentrate solely on the meaning of each vocabulary word, dismissing the different colors of text that appeared for every water-related term. He finally resorted to reading each sentence to himself in a whisper in a somewhat futile attempt to stop the colorful words from jumping off the screen. He alternated between the highlighter options of laser yellow, safety orange, day-glow green, and high-vis pink, hoping one of the neon colors would mask the other colors. It didn't really work. Casey plodded through the rest of the assignment at a snail's pace, praying the exam wouldn't cover much of this material…and, most of all, that the bell would ring soon.

* * * *

A few days later, Mandi Howe bounced up to Casey's desk before biology began. She beamed, her bright white smile contrasting with her dark skin tones. "We made the front page!" Excited, she thrust the paper in front of Casey's face. She placed her hands on her hips and looked down at the paper with pride. "It's a good picture of you if I must say so myself."

Casey's tight lips softened into a satisfied smile as he stared at the photo of him in the pool taken seconds after breaking the record. He had one arm resting on the lane line as he gave a wide, yet not entirely awkward, smile. Though his attempts to control his unruly head of wet hair had proved largely unsuccessful, at least the goggles hadn't left red indentation lines around his eyes that made him resemble a raccoon. Not bad, he thought, given the fact he was still catching his breath at the time, and his weary arms and legs had felt as heavy as bricks.

"The editor cut out the whole section about you 'reading the water,'" she added, glancing over his shoulder at her printed text, "so if you ever want to elaborate on that ability, I'm all ears."

"Oh…um, yeah," Casey stammered, his mouth dropping into an uncomfortable frown. After spending an enjoyable evening with Mandi, which he didn't really but sort of thought maybe had counted as an informal date, he wanted to help her out for her next story. Except for the fact that he still wasn't ready to share his unusually colored view of the water with everyone. News traveled too quickly around Westlake, and as far as Casey was concerned, the less people knew about his ability, the better. Wasn't a broken pool record enough to catch people's attention? Besides, if things went the way he planned tonight, his performance in this meet should be enough of a follow-up story as the team headed to Sections.

Mandi seemed to sense his reservation from his extended silence. She shrugged, and her lips turned up in a soft smile. "Well, maybe some other time," she suggested in a hopeful tone. "I'll be cheering for you from the stands." With a quick wave that made her curls bounce around her shoulders, she returned to her seat two rows in front of Casey and chatted with her friends until class began.

"What's with you and Casey?" her friend, Christina Loveland, leaned across the aisle to ask Mandi. Her long blonde hair fell from her shoulder, creating a veil around her round face that hid her expression from view.

Mandi turned to Christina, handing her the paper. She pointed to the large picture on the front page. "It's my latest story. Did you know he's trying out for the Olympics next year? That's right, *the* Olympics."

She answered just loud enough that Casey could catch every word.

Casey didn't bother to catch Christina's reply. Mandi's comment stung a little, giving him the uncanny feeling that she pretended to like him only to help out her promising future career in journalism. Twirling his pencil between his fingers, Casey mulled over this new development for the majority of the class period. Had she only asked him out for coffee in the hopes he would spill everything about his condition so she could spin that news into a juicy article to attract more readers? "Anything for a story," she had told him after he apologized for getting the bottoms of her jeans wet by the side of the pool. He kicked himself for misinterpreting her intentions. At least he had the sense to avoid mentioning his synesthesia condition. It didn't matter that doctors had also diagnosed several famous poets and composers with the same capabilities. People simply wouldn't understand and would think he was nuts.

It shouldn't have mattered. Casey had more than enough heaped on his plate at the moment. Still, he noticed that Mandi had made an effort to talk to him a few times in class, whereas before the interview, she had ignored him altogether. Casey wished he had more time to get to know her, but with the end of the season rapidly approaching, he was in crunch mode. So at the moment, other aspects of his life must wait.

The seconds ticked by at an extraordinary pace. Not until the final minutes of class did Casey realize he hadn't even begun his assignment. He chastised himself for getting distracted in the subject that was supposed to interest him the most.

After the doctor had diagnosed him with synesthesia, Casey grew fascinated with the workings of the human brain and aspired to become a neurosurgeon. He knew that wasn't the typical dream for a ten-year-old. At that age, most of his friends wished to be professional athletes, police officers, or video game designers.

His mom understood why the field of neuroscience and medicine interested him but reminded Casey the intensity of those careers wasn't for everyone. He didn't interpret her comment as a warning, rather as a lofty goal he sought to attain. Unfortunately, he was doing a pretty lousy job at the moment and letting the distractions cloud his ability to focus on the class.

Casey felt a huge sigh of relief when the period drew to a close. He intentionally didn't look up when the bell rang, pretending to be preoccupied with packing up his bag. In his periphery, he spotted Mandi leaving the class with her friends. Only then did he bother to head out of the room.

The rest of the day lagged. Casey felt relief when he grabbed his duffel bag and entered the locker room. He walked beneath the bright blue letters spelling *POOL* and opened the door, bombarded instantly with the aroma of homemade chocolate chip cookies mixed with the strong scent of chlorine.

Coach Harris caught him on the other side of the locker room door, dressed in his usual meet day attire of khaki shorts and navy blue Westlake High School polo. His shirt bore an embroidered logo of a ferocious wolf mascot with sharp, bared teeth in gold and white, above the words "SWIM AND DIVE." He adjusted the matching navy cap with a gold "W" on his head and looked down at his clipboard with his lineup for the meet. "Casey, I've made a few last-minute changes to your events. I know you're the favorite in the two hundred individual medley, especially after breaking the pool record last week, but I think Andrew can fill in for you there and still squeak out a win. I really need you to fill in somewhere else tonight, so I've decided to put you, Rohan, and Shawn in the one hundred backstroke instead."

Casey opened his mouth to object, then promptly closed it without uttering a word. He knew from experience not to argue. Coach Harris had won a few state championships in his day and knew what it took to succeed. Plus, disagreeing with him in the past had earned Casey nothing beyond a spot on the bench.

"Yes, Coach," he said, deliberately choosing the only affirmation his coach liked to hear.

"Good." Coach Harris gave a satisfied nod and drew a circle around Casey's name for the event. "Now go get ready," he said, closing his pen with a click. "I've heard the Storm's got a new powerhouse in the backstroke, and I think you're our best shot at neutralizing the threat."

"I'll try my best," Casey responded. He slung his duffel bag over his shoulder and made a beeline for his swim locker. Inside, he chuckled at how his coach's specific choice of words sounded more like a captain readying troops for war rather than someone trying to amp his swimmers up for a meet.

The backstroke was Casey's least favorite event. Keeping his head out of the water for the majority of the race proved a strong disadvantage in his ability to read the water. Instead of recognizing the colored currents, he had to rely strictly on his tactile sensation of feeling minor fluid differences through his fingertips. He'd only have a short glimpse of the water on each flip turn during those four lengths of the pool. Casey hoped those three quick glimpses would be enough.

On the way to his locker, Casey pondered which swimmer Coach Harris referred to as the "new powerhouse" from Great Plains High School. They had faced this team earlier in the season, and no one on their roster particularly stuck out in Casey's mind. *Guess I'll have to wait and see*, Casey thought, prepping his mind for this new mission.

* * * *

A couple of events before the one hundred backstroke, Casey began stretching out his arms and legs, keeping his muscles loose in his team warm-ups. He'd intently watched every previous race, expecting to find a new standout on the other team. But so far, no one seemed to fit Coach Harris's description of talent.

Finished with his stretches, Casey grabbed his gold "W" cap and goggles from his pocket and slipped off his team warm-ups to head over to the starting blocks. Out of habit, he looked into the stands to catch his mom's eye before the race. Normally she'd give him two thumbs-up in encouragement. Instead of finding his mom, he spotted Mandi Howe, who gave an excited wave. He noticed she had rolled her jeans above her knees today, which made him smile. He felt the blush rise up his cheeks and meekly returned her greeting.

Clear your head, he scolded himself, refusing to spend another minute dwelling on the thoughts that had consumed his mind during most of biology class. He reminded himself that he didn't have time for distractions.

Returning his focus to the upcoming race, Casey glanced to both sides of lane three to size up his competition. He'd raced his friends and teammates, Rohan Chopra and Shawn Frasier, several times throughout the year. Rohan's long arms and legs made him a strong backstroker, but Casey had greater endurance and grit that paid off over the course of this race. Shawn excelled in shorter races like the fifty yard freestyle, although Coach kept testing him in other races outside of his specialty. Rohan and Shawn were skilled athletes who possessed lots of untapped talent that would benefit the team in the future seasons. Still, Casey had competed with both of them for several years and felt confident he could beat them tonight.

He remembered two of the three swimmers on the Great Plains' swim team from their meet earlier in the season, but the swimmer in the adjacent lane four seemed new. His black Storm Swimming hoodie hung low over his eyes. Casey noticed the cord to his earbuds dangled freely out the front. Unlike the other backstrokers, he made no attempt to stretch or shake out his arms in the final moments before the race. Instead, he sat in the chair against the wall to his lane. His shoulders slumped forward in a casual, almost bored manner. Or perhaps he used this time for personal meditation? Regardless, Casey had to admit he'd never seen anyone act that way right before a race.

Could that be the powerhouse his coach had described? He reminded himself not to overthink the swimmer's actions or lack thereof; he didn't want to psyche himself out of the race. Relying on years of mental preparation, Casey trained his focus on his event, visualizing the entire race from start to finish in a matter of seconds.

Keeping his eyes locked on the lane before him, Casey began his pre-race ritual. He dipped his cap into the water and fitted it snugly across his thick hair, letting the refreshing water drench his body and stimulate his muscles. Satisfied with the cap's fit, he stretched the goggles' strap over his head, pressing the smooth plastic into his eye sockets for a good seal.

Casey cast a final glance at the swimmer next to him. He had shed his black hoodie, revealing a head of wispy, flaming red hair. He appeared long and lean with large hands and feet, which Casey thought would provide a definite advantage in moving quickly through the water…if they weren't paired with the swimmer's current sluggish movements as he lethargically strapped on his cap and mirrored goggles. Casey couldn't understand why his coach seemed so worried about this guy. He certainly didn't give the impression of stiff competition.

Unlike other individual events, the backstroke began in the water. One by one, the swimmers dove in, then returned to the starting blocks. Casey used this opportunity to let the water infuse his body with renewed strength, ready to unleash in a sudden burst of explosive speed. He casually entered the water, feeling the stream of bubbles slide across his chest. Opening his eyes underwater, he took a mental picture of the path of least resistance in green and stored it inside his memory. He broke through the surface for a breath, rolling his shoulders to loosen his muscles with each pull. He swam, looking up at the ceiling and counted the number of strokes until he hit the wall to settle his nerves.

Only when he neared the starting blocks did he notice the water seemed unusually warm, like a pocket of heat emanated from the adjacent lane. Startled, Casey paused mid-stroke and flipped onto his belly, searching for the cause.

He turned toward the source of the heat, never anticipating the view before him. Shocked, he thrashed backward, distancing himself from the underwater scene in lane four. The patch of warmth appeared to swirl, transforming into eddies of density currents where the cool water contacted the inexplicable, foreign heat.

Casey's jaw fell open, balking at the swimmer in the middle of the swirling, red mass of heat. He calmly bobbed in the water, completely unaware of the ongoing battle of temperatures around him. Casey stared in disbelief, watching the swimmer's skin gradually change color until he glowed bright orange, bathed in a haze of citrus steam.

CHAPTER THREE

Casey rubbed his fingers in his goggles to clear the lenses. Had he grabbed somebody else's pair off the bench by mistake? He snatched them from his head to check, surprised to see his familiar clear goggles. When he placed them back in position on his face, his view remained the same.

"Rohan," Casey whispered across the lane, "do you see anything weird?"

Rohan Chopra gave Casey an irritated shake of his head with a look that read, *Can't you see I'm busy getting ready for this race?* He made minor adjustments to his cap and goggles, deliberately ignoring Casey in the process.

Casey turned back to the swimmer from Great Plains in the lane next to him, careful to keep his mouth from gaping open again.

The swimmer caught his eye. Nonchalantly, he stuck out his hand in greeting. "Hey. Owen Teague." His mirrored goggles reflected the expression of shock written across Casey's face.

He squeaked out, "I'm Casey Donnelly," and returned the handshake. The instant his hand made contact with Owen,

Casey's eyes bulged with surprise. Owen's hand radiated intense amounts of heat, nearly scorching Casey's bare palm.

"Good luck to you, man," Owen said, retracting his grip.

Casey knew he should return his competitor's wish, only he didn't trust his voice to work. He stared at his hand with bewilderment, trying to ascertain why his palm continued to burn like he'd unwittingly placed his hand upon a hot stovetop. He quickly submerged his hand to dull the pain, but it didn't really help.

Shaking his head, Casey willed his mind back on track for this event. Four lengths of the pool. That was all. He could do this…if he could block out his confounding senses and focus on the task at hand. He took a deep breath and drove all distractions from his head, forcing himself to think of nothing beyond the next minute of his life.

Casey stretched his hands upward to grasp the backstroke handles set a few inches below the platform of the starting block. He planted his feet against the wall, twisting each slightly until his toes locked into the grout lines of the tiled pool, using friction to secure his feet in place. He forced his weight onto the ball of each foot to optimize his push at the sound of the buzzer.

The race announcer proclaimed, "Swimmers, take your marks."

Casey poised, ready to begin.

BEEEEEEP.

Casey sprang off the starting block, his feet driving him off the wall. He arced his back to enter the water in a streamlined position. Out of the corner of his eye, he caught a quick glimpse at Owen in the adjacent lane. Oddly, a bright orange glow still surrounded his competitor. He gasped with surprise, accidentally expelling some of his air too early. Casey cursed himself for his lack of focus and pumped his legs harder underwater to stay even with Owen. They surfaced in unison with Casey half a stroke behind. He took a quick breath to re-supply his depleted lungs, then began a series of long, deep pulls. Casey knew he'd have to work extra hard to regain position throughout the next three-and-a-half lengths of the pool.

The flags soon appeared overhead, marking the measured proximity to the wall. Casey counted his strokes, then rolled on his belly for a flip turn. He pumped his legs in a swift butterfly kick, this time surfacing an arm length in front of Owen.

His thumb exited the water faster, his upper arm brushing past his ear when his hand rotating at the top of each stroke. He focused on the mechanics of his stroke and maximizing his pull underwater. Casey's muscles burned with a buildup of lactic acid, but he pushed himself to dig deeper into his reserves. His legs kicked harder, driving him forward like a propeller on an outboard motor, refusing to relent.

Coach Harris gave the same words of advice to the team before every meet, and now those words echoed through his mind. "Hold nothing back. Live without regret." Casey adopted this mantra as a reminder of laying everything he had on the line, no matter how tired he felt during those brief seconds in the pool. The colored lane lines appeared once more, and Casey prepared for his second flip turn of the race.

He exited the wall, kicking fast. Casey noticed that he and Owen had pulled ahead of the rest of the heat, leaving a full body length between them and Rohan in third. But when he glanced at Owen's lane, he saw red eddies of water spiraling off his competitor's fingertips, leaving a long reddish trail down the middle of the pool.

The crowd cheered in the stands. Judging by their noise, they seemed completely oblivious to the red current trailing behind Owen.

Forget about it, he told himself. How many times had he seen or smelled or tasted something in the water that others couldn't detect? He had learned long ago to avoid sharing those observations with anyone. Still, it frustrated him whenever his synesthesia seemed to get the best of him.

One turn to go. He caught a glimpse of Coach Harris waving his cap in the air as he yelled at him from the side of the pool. Though he couldn't catch the words above the din of the crowd muffled in the swirling waters around his ears, he imagined him encouraging Casey to finish strong in his own brusque sort of way.

Coming out of the final flip turn, Owen and Casey raced neck and neck. Casey matched each stroke to his competitor's speed, refusing to let Owen pull ahead in the final sprint to the wall. Bolts of burning pain shot like lightning through his calf muscles as he held nothing back in kicking harder through the final lengths of the race. His arms seared white-hot all the way down to his fingers like fire infused his veins as he finished each stroke, but still, he willed them to move faster and dig deeper through the water. Using every last ounce of energy in his fatigued limbs, Casey's hand slammed into the touchpad.

He turned around, looking at the scoreboard for the instant display of results. "What was my time?" he gasped breathlessly, waiting for the results to appear.

The times flashed across the scoreboard, and Owen Teague threw his hands into the air, giving a jubilant wave to the audience. The crowd of Storm fans from Great Plains roared, their cheers echoing across the pool. Fuming, Casey pounded his fist into the water. Despite his excruciating effort, he had finished only two one-hundredths of a second behind.

He snapped his swim cap and goggles off his head and let the water spill off his body as he dragged himself out of the pool. His chest heaved with frustration while confusion muddled his mind. What had happened in that race? He was even with Owen for the entire four lengths. If only he hadn't let the unusual red and orange colors of the water distract him. Or the heat, he reminded himself. He had never experienced anything like that before in any of his previous competitions. What could explain the sudden change? Stress? Anxiety? He kicked himself for letting his mind drift away when he'd spotted Mandi in the stands before the start. He couldn't blame her, he realized. He let Owen's unexpected appearance in the water cloud his judgment instead of focusing solely on the race.

He kept his head low as he sulked toward the team bench, not even bothering to get eye contact with his coach or his mom in the stands. He suddenly felt a pocket of hot air brush alongside him.

"Hey. Good race, man," Owen said and congratulated him with a friendly pat on his back.

Casey's skin burned at the contact, making him recoil at Owen's touch. He glared at Owen, trying to figure out how he had this effect on him. In the overhead lights of the pool, a cardinal steam rose off the water that beaded across Owen's chest. The steam swirled around his head of spiky wet hair, surrounding his body in a hazy red glow, like the scattered rays of light when the sun sunk low on the horizon. When he swam outdoors in early summer, Casey had seen swimmers exit the water, leaving a trail of white steam rising off their bodies when their internal temperature differed greatly from the cool morning air. Yet the steam was always white, never the blazing colors of autumn leaves that danced around Owen.

"What's wrong with you?" Casey blurted, unable to contain his rising emotions. He stepped backward, eager to put distance between him and Owen with his bizarre source of heat.

Owen shrugged. He casually dragged his fingers through flaming ginger hair and flashed Casey an irritatingly wide grin. "Why do you look so surprised? I mean, sure, I may be outside my element, but what'd you expect? We can't all be a water elly like you." His grin opened into a full-blown chuckle. He put two fingers to his forehead in mock salute to Casey, then sauntered over to the Great Plains' team bench. Casey could hear him snickering to himself as he wandered away.

Casey stared at Owen in disbelief, his eyes narrowing with disdain. *Water elly?* What did that even mean? He'd heard all sorts of smack talk before races over the years, but this one completely stumped him. Why had Owen chosen that particular combination of words? Or was he just poking fun at Casey's surname, twisting and truncating "Donnelly" until it sounded like a derogatory term?

Still, something didn't make sense. Owen had no reason to razz him about his last name when he was the swimmer who had finished victorious. Plus, how did that explain the remarkable heat and red steam rising from his competitor? Casey didn't know how to react.

Casey pondered Owen's comment and actions the whole way back to the bench. He kept his eyes trained on his feet, hoping Coach Harris would be too preoccupied with the next race to notice Casey's return.

Unfortunately, Casey had no such luck.

Coach Harris stopped him en route. He placed a firm hand on Casey's shoulder to get his attention. "What happened out there? I thought you had him in the last few yards," Coach Harris said. Casey couldn't miss the disapproval in his tone.

He diverted his eyes from his coach's stern gaze. "I'm not exactly sure. I mean, the water changed temperature and color around him during the race, and I guess it distracted me."

"Changed color?" Coach Harris looked from the pool to Casey with disbelief. He dropped his hand from Casey's shoulder, his eyes growing cool with distrust. "What are you talking about?"

Casey frowned. He had made it this long without ever telling his coach about reading the colors in the water. Without that prior context, the question became more challenging to answer. "It's hard to explain." He released a deep sigh. Better to let it all spill out, he figured. Things couldn't get much worse at the moment. "Well," he started, hoping he had made the right choice in divulging his observations. "It's like he was, um, glowing red, I guess."

"That's impossible. A person can't 'glow red,'" Coach Harris guffawed. "He was just playing games with your head. Sure, this isn't your normal event, but I still think you could have taken him today. I know, it happens. You've been under a lot of pressure. We have a couple of weeks left. So train harder. And next time, don't let him get inside your head."

He nodded, giving his coach the perception of filing that information for future reference, then grabbed his towel to throw over his back and plopped down on the team bench, letting his head sink into his hands.

"Good race," Rohan congratulated him with a slap on his back.

Casey glanced up at Rohan and Shawn wrapped in towels, their hair wet and disheveled from the race. He gave them each a limp handshake. "Yeah, you too," he replied in a hollow voice, then let his head droop into his hands again. Why did he have to sense things that others could not? Every time he received the same reaction: people thought he had lost his mind.

He heard Shawn ask as his teammates walked away, "What's with him?"

He only caught a bit of Rohan's reply. It sounded something like, "New guy…only two one-hundredths…," but he missed the rest.

Casey sighed. It wasn't about the time. He had let the atypical colors and heat of a competitor distract him from complete focus during the race. What did it all mean? And what if it wasn't his synesthesia? He suddenly decided he needed another person's opinion about Owen. Someone impartial. Someone who had a good reason to speak to Owen…like for a short interview, perhaps.

Casey looked up and instantly spotted Mandi's brown curls and broad smile in the stands. He stared at her until he caught her attention, then waved her over.

She pointed at her chest. "Me?" she mouthed.

Casey nodded and gestured again for her to come over. She edged out of her seat and navigated the crowd of timers at each lane preparing for the upcoming race. No one would question her approaching the team bench, not when they all knew she wrote for the school paper.

"Sorry about the race," she said. Her lips turned down into a dejected frown. "I guess that sequel to the story will have to wait."

"Yeah," Casey agreed, though the newspaper article hadn't entered his thoughts. "Mandi, I need to ask you a favor. Can you find Owen, the guy who just beat me, and shake his hand? I want to see if you notice anything odd." His blue eyes held hers expectantly.

She crossed her arms. "You want me to do what?"

Casey wished he'd known Mandi longer than the past week, so this wouldn't seem like such an awkward request. But he had no choice. He had to discover the answer, and asking any of his teammates would arouse too much suspicion. "Can you pretend you're writing a story for the paper and ask him to take his picture?" he clarified. "Kind of like you did to me last week. Then when you shake his hand, tell me if anything seems…you know…*different*."

Mandi pinched her thin eyebrows. "I dunno. I probably should get going anyway. Big test tomorrow," she said, and glanced to the doublewide doors by the exit to the pool.

"Just wait," he blurted, realizing the look of avoidance inscribed in her expression. He hadn't wanted to share this information with anyone, but he needed her help. He could either abandon the whole issue or spill everything to her right now. He sighed, hoping he had made the right choice. Dropping his voice, he explained, "You told me before that you wanted to know the secret to my success. Well, here it is: the doctor said I have synesthesia."

Mandi took a surprised step backward, placing a careful distance between her and him.

He shook his head. "It's not contagious." He leaned closer so his teammates couldn't hear. "Synesthesia is a fusion of the senses from a cross-wiring in my brain. Some scientists think everyone may be born with it, but it disappears later in life when our senses become more specialized. Except I guess mine stayed linked, so sometimes I see colors in places other people can't. It's how I can read the water when I swim."

She exhaled a slow sigh of relief. "I never knew that was possible," she said. Her eyes had a faraway look, making Casey believe the gears in her mind were busily sifting through this new information and how to integrate it into her next piece for the paper.

"I'll explain more later," he said, interrupting her thoughts, "but right now, I need you to find Owen."

"Why? What does he have to do with this?" she wondered.

"Because this time, things were different," Casey explained quickly, eager to have her complete the task before Owen left the pool area. "This time, I read a *person*."

Mandi's gaze shifted from Casey to Owen and back.

"Can you just ask him? Please?" Casey begged. "I need to know if you sense anything different or if it was all in my head. He looked like he was glowing red."

"That's impossible," she said with a chuckle. "A person can't glow any color. He was just messing with your head. And obviously, it worked."

"I know, my coach told me the same thing," Casey replied. He let his head drop into his waiting hands with discouragement. He had disclosed more than he'd planned, and now she thought he was crazy on top of it all.

He felt a gentle hand against his shoulder and looked up to see Mandi's face lit in a sweet smile of reassurance. "Okay then, here goes," she said.

Casey watched her successfully meander her way across the pool deck as the next race began. Without hesitation, she walked right up to Owen and stuck out her hand in introduction. Owen accepted her offer but held her hand a little longer than Casey might have liked.

Her animated face lit while Casey guessed she explained her role at the school paper. When she playfully tossed her brown curly hair over one shoulder, Casey could tell she laughed at Owen's comment. Possibly about Casey and the "water elly" remark, for all he knew. "Well, that really backfired," Casey muttered to himself as their conversation lasted far longer than he had anticipated.

A few minutes later, Mandi waved goodbye to Owen and weaved her way around the timers and race officials to return with her report. "Owen just moved here from Phoenix a month ago. He said he isn't quite used to the cold yet. But otherwise, nothing out of the ordinary as far as I could tell. Large hands, firm grip," Mandi noted, the blush rising in her cheeks as she spoke. "But really, a normal handshake." She shrugged at Casey. "What did you expect me to notice?"

"Nothing else," Casey lied. Maybe Coach Harris was right, and he had merely imagined the whole thing. He stood up and forced his lips into a smile. "Thanks again for your help. I should probably get ready for my next race now," he said.

Mandi's warm brown eyes cooled like the crisp air that preceded the first flakes of snow, but before she could reply, Casey walked away without a glance behind. He found his water bottle and gulped huge mouthfuls, hoping the liquid would wash away the burn of frustration that inflamed his throat and help him forget about Owen's water ellies so he could focus on his next race.

Out of the corner of his eye, he saw Mandi shake her head of bouncy curls before leaving the team bench, her hands resting on her hips with irritation. A part of Casey wondered if his sudden change had puzzled her, but the other part decided he couldn't let it bother him, not when he had other concerns to worry about.

Instead, he mulled her facts over in his mind. If Owen had just moved here from Phoenix as Mandi had claimed, that would explain why Casey hadn't seen him the last time their teams had met and why Coach had called him the "new powerhouse." Still, the reddish colors of water and steam that flowed around Owen's body made absolutely no sense.

Casey spent the rest of the meet in a daze, only coming out of it long enough to finish a strong race and avoid further ire with Coach Harris. At the conclusion of the meet, Casey eagerly returned to the locker room and changed at lightning speed, skipping the shower to answer the question that plagued his mind. He carelessly tossed everything into his bag, then exited the locker room with his phone in hand. Once outside, he found a quiet corner of the hallway where he Googled Owen's taunt, *water elly*.

His phone wrote, *Did you mean water belly?* A collection of images of flotation devices for the pool popped up, followed by the Facebook profiles of a few women with variations of the name, "Elly Water."

Casey stuffed his phone into his pocket. That search didn't help at all.

Was the nickname simply a play off his last name, Donnelly? Or Owen's version of a twisted, cruel joke to psyche out his competition? Because Casey was starting to believe that Owen's plan had worked in effectively breaking into Casey's mind.

Nothing made any sense. Casey threw on his jacket and hat, picked up his bags with a huff, and headed for the parking lot, feeling more confused than ever.

* * * *

Every quarter at school, Casey enrolled in visual arts classes, completing the assignments required for class in the style his teachers suggested. But at home, his artwork took an entirely different approach. At home, he painted the colors of the water as only he saw them. His mom called it "abstract art," while Grandma Louise said his work was a form of "art therapy." Casey didn't bother to correct either.

He had only hung one painting as decoration in his room: his favorite of the collection. This piece depicted a background of blocky, overlapping rectangles of blue and green with a swirling crimson path trailing into the distance. In the upper right hand corner, he placed a single splotch of bright daffodil yellow.

To the casual observer, the canvas might have resembled a single flower planted at the end of a long, winding path through a grassy field. But Casey knew the inspiration for this work came from a terrible reminder of the day he had almost lost his cousin. The day when the rip current, flashing like a blood red rush of water, had dragged Jason far out to sea along the Carolina coast. The day when Casey had first acknowledged his alarming differences. And the day that had begun a whole new chapter in his life.

Not only had he discovered a natural talent he'd never anticipated, he'd also learned to filter his thoughts and speak only what others expected to hear. Casey saw things outside the realm of ordinary; his mother's worrisome expression made that abundantly clear. Water wasn't supposed to change color. Words in a textbook should look black and white.

Even though the doctor assured Casey that others with synesthesia could fuse their senses through artistic outlets like poetry or other visual arts, Casey still felt different from the stories he read about his condition. His senses always blended in a predictable way, but only under specific circumstances. Over time, he noticed a recurring trend.

Unlike others with synesthesia who might see a splotch

of magenta whenever they take a bite of sirloin steak or feel a brush of wind against their face when they hear the melody of a flute, Casey never experienced any of these symptoms. He never saw the days of the week fall into a pattern like the spokes on a wagon wheel or sensed a quick stab of pain when he saw the color orange.

For Casey, connections between his senses only occurred with water. During class, whenever he heard a student stop for a drink at the water fountain at the end of the hall, the same sweet taste of apple pie topped with whipped cream would fill his mouth. Casey knew he shouldn't be able to detect such a small sound so far away, but for some reason, he did.

When he read the classic novel *Moby Dick*, nearly every word jumped off the page in brilliant Technicolor, like opening credits for a television movie. Every time the word "water" showed up in turquoise blue like the gemstones of the American Southwest, but "sea" stood out as a deep pink, resembling the fuchsia flowers in the hanging baskets at his Grandma Louise's lake home.

At school, all the signs for the main office, library, and computer labs were written in bold black capital letters, yet the sign at the entrance to the pool appeared in shimmering sapphire blue every time it welcomed him through its doors. And each time he entered, he smelled homemade chocolate chip cookies overpowering the strong scent of chlorine, just like he'd walked into the comfort and security of his own home.

His "abstract" paintings allowed him a safe outlet to record his memories, especially since he'd stopped sharing his perceptions with others long ago. No one else saw the lap lanes quite like he did during his races. Navigating the teenage years in high school proved hard enough; Casey didn't dare stand out as an oddity on his team. He kicked himself for confiding in Coach Harris and Mandi at the meet that evening. Telling them hadn't helped his situation one bit; in fact, it might have made matters worse.

In one corner of his room, Casey kept his pile of paintings stacked in a neat pile. His mom would've hung the entire collection on every wall in their house if he'd let her, but Casey didn't want his friends to know how many he'd painted over the years. Casey thought boys his age were supposed to spend their free time occupied with other activities like playing sports, video gaming, or hanging out with friends after school. Not obsessing over the nuances of color gliding off his fingers with a single freestyle pull.

"Well, maybe it's not exactly 'obsessing,'" Casey muttered to himself. "It's just an outlet for me to express myself since I can't share my thoughts." He knew no one would understand.

He only permitted Grandma Louise to select whichever paintings she wanted to hang up at her home. It really didn't matter since none of his friends ever went with him to visit her at the lake.

Casey flipped through a few of his finished canvases, trying to push Owen's "water elly" taunt to the back of his mind as he searched for any resemblance to the image following today's race. One canvas depicted dozens of mint green and pale yellow spheres, decreasing in size as they faded into the deep blue background. His mom thought they looked like miniature worlds in the cosmos. Casey simply nodded. The bubble trail off his fingertips when he broke through the surface of his dive had inspired that piece, but he knew she would tell him bubbles were supposed to appear translucent or white underwater, not the colors of chewing gum.

Another canvas showed vertical lines at steep angles in thick, bold hues of pumpkin orange, ruby red, and lemon yellow. His mom said she liked the flashes of color that reminded her of car taillights captured in time-delay photography on a darkened street. Casey agreed, knowing the real reason he had painted that picture. One day, a sudden downpour soaked him on his walk home from school. The miserable cold spring rain would have turned to snow if the temperature had dropped only a couple of degrees. He sloshed through deep puddles, adding to his misery as his wet toes turned numb. Completely drenched, he grumped to himself the entire mile and a half, furious his locker had jammed after dismissal. By the time he succeeded in opening the lock, he had already missed the bus.

By far, his favorite pieces of art focused on the swirling eddies and underwater vortices of his races when contrasting shades of complementary colors warred on the canvas: orange vs. blue or red against green. For Casey, shades and tints of greens and blues portrayed the feelings of safety and peace, while oranges and reds elicited a sense of unsettling fear. Still, none of these prior works quite mimicked the sight he had witnessed today during his race.

Casey opened a new canvas from one of the packs his mom had stockpiled from the arts and crafts store's discount summer sales. She bought several multi-packs to "fuel his creativity," she claimed. Even she didn't think of it as an obsession, but more like a hobby, he reminded himself, trying to simmer the rising anger and confusion he'd felt since the start of that backstroke race.

Casey set the canvas on his easel to secure it in place and opened his toolbox, where he stored his collection of acrylic paints. He preferred these to other types of media for their quick drying speed, which allowed him to finish the entire painting quickly while the sensations and emotions stood fresh in his mind. He twisted the cap of cerulean blue and squeezed the tube, leaving a large glob of paint on his palette that resembled the color of a shallow tropical sea. He followed with a dab of Windsor blue, a dark navy like the midnight sky. Then he added some faded antique white, sometimes mixing the paints on his palette and other times intentionally let the colors blend on the canvas as the mood fit. The soft, swirling colors fused together in swift brushstrokes as he filled the entire left and right sides of his canvas. He smiled, satisfied with his effort. The undulating pattern reminded him of the "good water," or his path of least resistance, just like he remembered the scene from his race. He washed out his brushes with soap and water, then let the paint dry. If he added the other colors now, they would mix into an unpleasant shade of mud.

After finishing dinner, a shower, and most of his homework, Casey returned to his painting. The bright red light on his clock warned him of the late hour and how he needed his rest. But Casey figured trying to sleep now would prove pointless, and he doubted his memory would be this clear in the morning. He knew he'd feel much better once he completed his task and set his mind at ease. Especially when Owen's "water elly" jibe repeated over and over in his mind.

Casey squeezed his eyes tight, letting Owen's irritating retort fuel his creative energies. He painted with vigor in furious strokes, unleashing the pain and humiliation he felt from the race in great splashes of cardinal red and cadmium yellow. The colors blended to create a vivid orange across the middle. He ignored the passing minutes on the clock, letting his mind calm as the paints filled every gap until no sections of blank canvas remained.

His emotions finally diffused, Casey stepped back to admire his work. At a close range, the textured brush strokes felt fast and angry. But from a distance, the painting took on an entirely different form.

"No way," Casey breathed. A low whistle escaped his lips.

In the center of cool, calming waters stood a searing trail of wildfire, cleaving the canvas in half.

Casey blinked, stunned by his creation. Unmistakable tongues of flames erupted in the middle, just like Owen had blazed his way past Casey in the backstroke. He stared at the painting, suddenly realizing why none of his other creations had captured the feelings he'd experienced today.

He had never painted fire before. He always painted water.

Always.

A renewed resolve filled his mind. More than ever, Casey was determined to find Owen Teague, who owed him an explanation.

CHAPTER FOUR

After Casey had passed his road test a few months ago, his mom agreed that he could borrow the car whenever it didn't conflict with her schedule. Still, he felt like he was hiding something from her when he asked to meet a friend after practice at Great Plains High School. Even though she readily consented, Casey felt a wave of guilt wash over him. He hadn't shown his mom his latest painting on purpose. And Owen Teague wasn't exactly what he'd call a "friend."

Casey staged himself at the exit from the locker room, hoping he had made it in time. He recognized a couple of swimmers with their wet shiny hair poking out from under their caps, the ends characteristically lightened into shades of gold from the effects of spending months in heavily chlorinated waters. He watched each pass, making sure he hadn't missed Owen by mistake. A few minutes passed before Owen walked out the door, his backpack slung over one shoulder and his black hood thrown up, obscuring most of his red hair hanging low over his eyes. Casey chided himself for thinking he wouldn't recognize the guy. Why wouldn't he when a noticeable orange colored steam, like the smoldering embers of a campfire left unattended, emanated from the strands of damp hair under his hood?

Owen's head slumped forward, his gaze focused on his phone when he suddenly jerked upright like he had sensed Casey's presence. He stowed his phone in the front pouch of his black Storm swim team hoodie. "What? Miss me already?" he joked, his smile widening until it exposed all of his teeth. "Hashtag, 'Spy much'?"

"Huh?" Casey's right eyebrow perched high on his forehead, nearly reaching his hairline.

Owen ran his fingers through his hair to move the long strands away from his eyes. "You couldn't wait until our next meet? Had to check out the competition beforehand?" he continued.

"Oh, that," Casey mumbled, feeling his cheeks grow warm. His hands dug deep into his pockets and fumbled with his keys. Since their last race, Owen's mysterious comment had consumed his thoughts during every waking moment. Casey had made the effort to come all the way over here for an explanation but now felt at a strange loss for words. Just spit it out, he scolded himself. "No, not exactly," he said. "To be honest, I had a question for you."

"Really?" Owen chuckled, his hazel eyes lit with surprise. "Okay, shoot."

Casey closed his eyes, visualizing the blaring conflagration of reds and yellows through a serene background of blue-green, cleaving the calm waters of his canvas in two. He opened his eyes and looked straight into Owen's gaze, voicing the question that stood foremost in his mind. He took a deep breath, then began. "After the one hundred backstroke, you said something to me that I've been thinking about ever since."

Owen gave a knowing nod. "Go on."

"Well, I don't really get what you meant when you called me a 'water elly.' Is it a play off my last name or something?"

Owen chortled, his cutting laughter echoing throughout the vacant halls. "That's what's gotten under your skin? You came all the way over here to find me to ask me about ellies?" One side of his smile curled like it mocked the simplicity of Casey's question.

"Ellies?" Casey tried to hide the confusion in his voice. It didn't really work.

"Well, sure. You didn't think you were the only one, did you?" It almost sounded like Owen had refrained himself from adding a mocking, "duh," at the end of his sentence.

"What do you mean?" Casey asked, feeling stupid for sounding as clueless as he did at the moment.

"Here. Check this out, dude." Owen waved Casey nearer and whipped out his phone. He typed a few words into the search bar and pulled up a YouTube video.

Casey leaned over Oven's shoulder to better see the screen. "Who's that?" he asked.

"Mason Brown," Owen said in a tone that suggested, *obviously*.

Casey scrunched his nose. "Mason, who?"

"Aw, c'mon. You haven't heard of him yet? Well, you will soon. He's gonna be a legend. Here, watch this." Owen edged the phone toward Casey.

The video started out with Mason's name, high school, and list of events. Casey had seen ones like this before: prospect videos to generate a buzz with college recruiters. He wondered if it was a bad thing that he hadn't created one for himself yet. He made a mental note to ask his mom to video all of his races from now on so he'd have some footage to use in the future.

Next, the prospect video zoomed in on Mason positioning his feet on the starting blocks of the track. The camera panned out to include the whole track. A bright yellow circle outlined Mason's form, dressed in his school colors of white and red, against the other sprinters in his heat. At the sound of the gun, they took off in a collective blur. Within seconds, Mason had pulled ahead of his competition, widening the gap with each speedy stride. He thrust his chest forward when he crossed the finish line, then threw his arms high in the hair with jubilation. A massive grin spread across his face as he waved to the cheering crowd.

"So? He's got talent," Casey noted, wondering what this guy had to do with Owen's comment about "ellies."

"No, no, no, man. You've gotta watch this next part," Owen said. He gave Casey a quick nudge in the ribs with his elbow as a reminder to keep his attention focused on the screen.

In the next sequence, the videographer flashed to a second clip of Mason. Judging by the lighting and background scenery, Casey could tell this race occurred on an entirely different day and at a different venue. The camera followed Mason to the start of the race.

"Here it is. Watch this." Owen sounded giddy with excitement. He pushed the phone closer to Casey with anticipation.

As Mason walked past the long jump pit, he bent down and picked up a handful of sand. He stood back up and held the sand close to his face, almost like he inhaled a deep breath of its scent, then let the rest of his handful scatter into the wind.

"Yes!" Owen cheered and pumped his fist to hammer home his point. He eagerly nodded his head, letting his long damp hair fall back into his eyes.

This wasn't helping at all, Casey realized with dismay. He cast a quick glance at Owen, afraid to let his eyes linger from the screen for too long in case he had missed an important part. "So what? That's no big deal," Casey admitted, unimpressed.

"But get this. He does the same thing before *every* race," Owen countered.

"So do I," Casey said with an indifferent shrug, thinking about his pre-race ritual of filling his cap with water, then dumping it over his head, shaking out his arms, and jumping up and down exactly three times. "Lots of athletes are superstitious. Once they find something that works, they stick with it. Sometimes, it's a lucky pair of socks they refuse to wash or refusing to shave their beards during a winning streak."

"No, you don't understand," Owen continued, his eyes still intently watching his cell phone.

Casey peered down at the screen. Mason lined up at the blocks for his next race, a yellow circle again tracing around his form to single him out from the others in his heat. The runner's muscles tightened, ready to spring into action like a coil suddenly unleashed at the sound of the gun start. "It's like he's drawing energy from the earth itself before he starts each event," Owen explained.

Skeptical, Casey raised a solitary eyebrow. "Have you ever bothered to ask Mason why he performs that ritual before each of his races?"

Owen quickly glanced at Casey with an uncomfortable smile. "Well, no. I haven't."

Casey crossed his arms over his chest. "So you've got no proof."

On the video, Casey heard the crack of a gunshot announcing the start of the race. His eyes instinctively fell back to the screen, where he watched Mason fly out of the starting blocks at lightning speed. In no time, he had again won the race by several paces in front of his closest competition.

"*There's* my proof," Owen said triumphantly.

"Uh huh," Casey replied in a doubtful tone, still a nonbeliever.

"It's not just Mason, though," Owen added. "You see it all the time in the pros. Like the Seahawks' quarterback, Dion Wilson, and the youngest pro-golfer to ever win the Masters, Jaden Donahue."

Casey didn't recognize any of the names. Between swimming and school—and his painting hobby, which he'd rather not mention to anyone, especially not Owen or his friends at Westlake—he didn't really have time to follow professional sports. "I'm still not sure what you're talking about. What does all of this have to do with 'ellies'?" he asked, hoping Owen might actually tell him what the term means.

"If you watch them long enough, you can recognize the signs," Owen explained.

"Signs? What signs?"

A wide grin filled Owen's face. "Trust me. You can't miss them."

Casey made a mental note to pay closer attention to sports on TV and maybe to go back and rewatch Mason Brown's prospect video again in case he had missed some sort of clue. Still, he hadn't gained any knowledge of value to help ease his mind. With a frustrated sigh, he decided to ask Owen directly. "Y'know, I still don't get why you called me an 'elly.' It's not like I'm in the same league as the pros."

"Not yet, at least," he amended, pointing his index finger in the air. "We've all got to start somewhere."

"*We?*" Casey exclaimed, embarrassed to admit his voice cracked slightly with surprise. "So what are you saying? That *you're* an elly, too?"

Suddenly, it didn't matter that he still couldn't decipher the meaning of that word. Somehow knowing that Owen was also an elly took all the mockery out of the word. Maybe Casey had misinterpreted his meaning. Maybe Owen intended his remark to sound informative rather than taunting after the race. He had just complimented Casey a moment ago that his swimming career held potential, and that had to count for something, especially from the toughest competition he'd seen all season.

Owen chortled with amusement. "Don't tell me you didn't notice I was a fire elly?" he asked, his voice incredulous.

A fire elly? The image of Casey's most recent painting flashed through his mind. The radiating heat and bright colors he'd felt and seen in the water made so much more sense if

Owen actually associated himself with fire. "Well, yeah," Casey admitted. "I mean, I guess it was pretty obvious." He remembered the shock he'd felt when Owen exited the pool, and his entire body glowed, encircled in a steamy red haze. Whatever it was, he wasn't alone. Owen had some connection with fire, just like his draw to water, and Mason's still unproven tie to the sand pit before each race. He paused for a moment before asking, "Are there many others around here?"

"Absolutely. At your school, there's the basketball phenom, Lee McCormick. But in the area, we also have rising hockey star, Taylor Sperry; tennis All-State, Flora Fernandez; and the soon-to-be-legendary sprinter you just saw on YouTube, Mason Brown," Owen explained.

Casey blinked. "Taylor?" He hadn't seen her since they attended Spring Hill elementary school together, but Taylor Sperry's picture appeared in the local paper almost every week for her impressive contributions to her hockey team.

"You know her? Then you must've realized she's a perfect example of an ice elly," Owen said.

Casey shook his head with disbelief. Not someone like Taylor. Sure, she loved hockey, but that didn't mean there was anything making her different from the other girls on the team. Though he still hadn't figured out what an Owen meant by the term, "elly," he knew one thing for certain: Taylor wasn't anything like Owen.

Over his years of training, Casey had learned that swimming was both physically and mentally demanding, and he assumed the same held true in other sports. Owen's previous compliment quickly fled from his mind, replaced instead with a growing conviction that since Casey possessed the physical competitiveness that threatened Owen's success, his competitor had to resort to other means to break down Casey's mental toughness through head games. And unfortunately for Casey, Owen's head games had started to work.

"There's no way. Taylor's just really good," Casey said, dismissing the thought. The doctors had diagnosed him with a logical explanation: his senses were fused like others with synesthesia, nothing more. "You know what I think? That you've got too much time on your hands, and you're reading into this 'elly' stuff way too much. I need to focus and get my mind back on track so I'll be ready for States, or there won't be a shot at the Olympic Trials for me."

"You don't believe me? Go and watch her some time," Owen challenged, his hazel eyes flashing from under his hood. "You'll see." He gave Casey an irritating wink and turned on his heels. A few paces down the hall, he called over his shoulder, his lips twisted on one side into a smirk. "Until next time, water elly."

Casey was sure Owen's smirk erupted into full-throated laughter as soon as he rounded the corner out of view, though he wasn't sure if the laughter stemmed from his own ignorance or his potentially foiled shot at the Trials. Worse, Owen had used that same nickname again: water elly. This time, despite everything he'd said about being an elly himself, Casey couldn't mistake his demeaning intent.

* * * *

Frustrated his visit to Great Plains had yielded more questions than answers, Casey decided to follow up on some of Owen's claims about other "ellies" in the area. Although he didn't know Lee McCormick personally since they didn't share any classes, he needed to test Owen's theory. After swim practice the following day, Casey joined some fans in the stands to watch the varsity basketball practice, remaining in his spot even after the rest of the bystanders and team managers had departed. He sat unnoticed in the upper corner of the stands, his eyes trained on Lee in his gold and navy practice jersey with a logo of a wolf's head on the front. He continued to practice his shots long after the team had called it quits for the night and headed to the locker room, turning off the main gym lights on their way out the door. Casey sunk into the shadows high in the bleachers, grateful no one had noticed his presence. He tried to shake the unsettling feeling that Owen's crazy ideas had turned him into a stalker, all in an attempt to discern the truth about his competitor's claims.

"It's got to be the extra time and effort," Casey whispered to himself, evident in the passion Lee devoted to the sport and his athletic commitment to stay long after everyone else had left. That hardly differed from Casey's dedication to swimming over the years. The extra time and energy he poured into the sport had helped him rise as one of the leaders on the Westlake Varsity team.

Sure, Lee sank nearly every shot he'd taken at practice, but the defense had blocked some of his attempts. Meanwhile, others had teetered on the edge before slowly dropping from the basket or swirled around like a toilet bowl threatened to suck down the contents before the ball mysteriously popped out without scoring any points.

Owen might counter that Lee intentionally influenced his shots to avoid arousing suspicions of the origin of his talent. But Casey understood the truth: Lee was good. Plain and simple. Something anyone could achieve with Lee's level of drive and passion for the sport.

Plus, he'd paid enough attention in biology to learn that genetics could play a part in his success. Lee stood about six-two or six-three, he guessed, which was a huge asset in this sport. Just like Mason Brown's long legs proved an advantage on the track, he might also have other genetic factors like a higher concentration of fast-twitch muscles, better suited for quick bursts of speed. Casey remembered reading an article his coach recommended about how to improve your speed and endurance and how the genetic makeup of fast-twitch to slow-twitch muscles could make an athlete more adept at sprints than long-distance races. At any rate, that explanation seemed much more sound than Owen's belief that inhaling dust from the sand pit enabled Mason to blow ahead of his competition.

Casey heard Lee's dribble slow to a rhythmic *tap, tap, tap* as Lee casually dribbled the ball across the court on his way to the locker room. He glanced around as if checking to make sure none of his teammates had returned to the gymnasium floor. Then at half court, he lobbed the ball backwards over his head in a blind shot in the general direction of the basket. The orange globe sailed through the air in a sweeping arc before beginning its descent.

Casey's jaw dropped with utter astonishment as he watched the ball drop toward the net. He couldn't believe Lee's accuracy with a random behind-the-back shot.

Lee turned to catch the end result of his toss just as the basketball swooshed through the net without even grazing the rim. The ball bounced a few times on its way back toward center court.

Lee pumped his fist with internalized excitement, then waited for the rebound to reach him. With a covert smile, he picked up the ball and set it on the rack by the exit door.

Unable to contain his amazement, Casey bounded down the bleacher steps two at a time, his footsteps sounding like echoing drums of thunder against the empty gymnasium walls. Lee paused and glanced up at the resounding noise, the blood quickly draining from his flushed face.

"That was incredible!" Casey exclaimed, leaping the final two steps to reach the gymnasium floor. "How'd you do it?"

"Huh?" Lee blinked, his dark eyes registering Casey with reserve and hesitation.

"I mean, it looked like you just tossed the ball over your shoulder like no big deal, and then you sank it. I mean, it didn't even hit the rim."

"Just luck, I guess," he replied, forcing his shoulders into a nonchalant shrug. A new layer of sweat beaded across his short black hair and dark forehead, for which Casey suspected his sudden, unexpected appearance in the gym was to blame. "Like you said, it was no big deal." Lee palmed the basketball in one hand, resting it against his abdomen as if creating a barrier between him and Casey.

Casey recognized his expression of discomfort, much like he'd felt toward Owen after their race. "I'm Casey Donnelly," he introduced himself, looking up to meet Lee's gaze. "I know you don't know me, but I swim here at Westlake. And I've gotta ask you a question."

Lee shifted his weight to his other foot, wordlessly waiting.

"Okay, see, I just met this guy from Great Plains who seemed a whole lot different than anyone I'd ever raced against before," Casey said, talking fast. He decided to omit the whole part about changing the temperature and color of the water and skip right to the end. "Anyway, he told me that I could notice these differences because I was a water elly and he was a fire elly. But I'm still so confused about what he means. And then he mentioned your name. He said that you were—"

"Let it go," Lee interrupted, a strong note of caution in his tone. "You said your name was Casey, right? I've heard your name on the student news a few times. You're a pretty decent swimmer, from what it sounds like."

Casey's modest eyes flicked to his feet before he responded. "Yeah, I guess so."

"Well, let me tell you, it's not worth ruining your life over. Your career, your future. It's just not worth it." Lee squared his jaw, his black eyebrows narrowed with conviction. He started to walk away with long strides, leaving Casey alone on the court.

"What do you mean? How would it ruin my future?" he called after Lee's departing form. A sudden rush of wind ruffled Casey's hair, probably from the start of the gymnasium fans' circulation cycle.

"Just forget it, man," Lee hollered back and burst through

the gymnasium door, letting it slam loudly in his wake.

Casey stood there in silence, pondering. The wise part of him knew he should heed Lee's advice, but the other daring and somewhat reckless side of his personality begged to know more.

CHAPTER FIVE

Casey's mind continually replayed his conversations with Owen and Lee over the next few days. As remarkable as Lee's performance had appeared, Casey decided he needed more proof, and the suggestion of a familiar name stuck in his head, providing the best way he could discern the truth behind Owen's "water elly" comment.

He pulled out his phone and checked her team's website. The schedule said the Falcons had a home game tomorrow. He'd head over to the game right after practice. That way, he could finally know for sure.

Casey arrived at the start of the third period, finding an inconspicuous spot high in the bleachers behind a few of the Eastlake fans dressed in black and green jerseys with a giant falcon clutching a hockey stick in its sharp, yellow talons. He intentionally removed his navy blue and gold Westlake swimming jacket before entering the rink to avoid drawing unwanted attention from his high school's cross-town rival, choosing to wear a plain gray long sleeve with his jeans instead. While he settled into his seat, he caught a few of the fans' comments on the game. Apparently, Eastlake was up two to one after Taylor had scored their second goal to take the lead.

Casey recognized Taylor instantly. She had tied her long jet black hair into a ponytail that trailed down the back of her white and green jersey, swaying back and forth with each stride, right through the middle of her lucky number twenty-eight. With his busy swimming schedule, he hadn't had the time to catch any hockey games this season, so he couldn't compare her performance to the Westlake girls' team. But from his perspective, he thought Taylor played flawlessly, gliding past her opponents with ease. Her crisp, leading passes landed right on her teammates' sticks every time. She carried the puck with quick feet and skated even faster without it as she jockeyed for position, showcasing her skill and competitiveness on the ice.

Casey watched the remainder of the game, not altogether surprised when her team took a commanding lead. Better yet, Taylor had earned an assist on each of the Falcons' next three goals. She celebrated each with a group hug on the ice, then skated past the team bench for high-fives, a satisfied smile painted across her face.

Still, Casey wasn't convinced. Taylor Sperry had been skating as soon as she learned how to walk. Like many kids in Minnesota, she had started playing hockey in preschool, one of the reasons his home had earned the nickname, "The State of Hockey."

The only way to know for sure was to ask her personally. He wasn't sure she'd recognized him since he'd shot up a few feet since he last saw her when they graduated from fifth grade, but she'd probably still remember his name, especially since they were in the same class for all of elementary school.

He leaned up against the glass lining the boards of the rink, waiting for her to exit after the game. Casey spotted her right away. Dressed in matching black team jackets and hockey pants with jersey numbers embroidered in emerald thread across their shoulders, Taylor headed out the door with one of her teammates, chatting excitedly as they relived their favorite moments of the game. A few young fans decked in black and green Falcons hockey apparel bounced on their heels and held out their hands for high-fives and fist bumps as the girls passed.

Taylor's long black hair, damp with sweat, fell flat against her face, parted on the side of her forehead. Her exertion during the game had left her cheeks rosy and flushed. She walked hunched over under the burden of a massive gear bag on her left shoulder and carried a pair of matching sticks in her right. A trace of a giddy smile remained on her lips, largely replaced with mounting fatigue from the energy expended during the game. And rightfully so: in their five to one win against the number one ranked team in the district, Taylor had walked out with four points: three assists plus the game-winning goal. She'd definitely played a huge role in her team's upset tonight.

"Hey, Taylor," Casey called, giving an amiable smile and wave. "Great game tonight." Despite how long it had been since he last saw her, he hoped she might recognize him.

"Thanks," Taylor automatically replied. She raised her hand halfway to wave back to him, then stopped frozen in her tracks. She paused and gazed at his face, her head tipped slightly to one side, likely from the weight of the gear bag, he assumed. "I'll see you later," she told her teammate. The girl smiled and gave her an understanding nod before walking past them.

Casey felt encouraged to know she did, in fact, recognize him. He took a step toward her, his blue eyes brightening.

"What are you doing here?" she asked, her voice laced with a hint of disdain. Her eyebrows pinched together as her gaze transformed instantly into a glare.

Surely she wasn't still upset about that little incident back in the fourth grade? No one could hold a grudge that long, he figured, and took another step closer so no one else could hear. He dropped his voice and said, "I had to see you. I've got a question for you, one I think only you can answer."

Her eyes darted nervously from one side to the other as

if desperate for an escape. "O-kay," she dared, her slow voice proceeding with caution.

Casey deliberately ignored every instinct in his body, telling him to try again another time. She obviously wasn't thrilled to see him here tonight. Still, she was the only chance he had to figure out if Owen was just messing with his mind. He had to know the truth before he faced Owen again in the pool. He needed to move on with his life and focus on his upcoming races, not these head games that consumed his thoughts. He couldn't wait for a better day to find her. He had to act now.

Swallowing hard, Casey leaned toward her, so his low voice brushed against her ear. "What do you know about ellies?"

Taylor leapt a step backward, her eyes cutting into his like daggers. Her rosy cheeks suddenly bleached stark white, resembling the color of baking flour. She bit her lower lip to silence its quivering, then replied in a deadpan voice, "I haven't got a clue what you're talking about." Without another word, she bolted past him, abruptly banging into his shoulder with her bulky gear bag, knocking him into the glass and boards surrounding the rink.

Casey rubbed the back of his head where it had hit the glass, wondering what he had said to make her so upset. Even if someone had overheard him, which he didn't think was at all possible since he had whispered the question directly into her ear, nothing in his spoken words revealed any information or accusations about her possible abilities. How could it, when he still didn't understand the meaning himself? He had to try again, he told himself. Judging by her frosty reaction, she knew exactly what he was talking about, and he felt desperate to learn more.

He ran out the doors after her, not even bothering to throw on his hat or gloves. His feet skidded and half-slid over the icy patches of the sidewalk to match her hurried pace. "Taylor, wait," he called, waving one hand in the air to draw her attention, but she kept walking with measured steps despite the poor conditions. Though the brisk wintry wind may have robbed his voice from reaching her ears, Casey got the sinking suspicion she deliberately chose to ignore him.

He willed his feet to shuffle faster across the slippery surface, wondering how she didn't seem to have any difficulty in widening the gap between them. "Taylor, please. I just need to talk to you for a minute," he tried again, his voice bordering on a shout to be heard. "There's something I need to know, and I thought you might be able to help me out."

Casey thought he heard her mutter something like, "Not again," before she spun on her heels, a sudden gust of wind whipping her long, black hair against her cheeks. Her pale blue eyes pierced his with a coldness that rivaled the frigid night air. "What is it with you?" she spat. "Why can't you take a hint and leave me alone?" she panted with mounting fury, her livid breath hanging in white frosted clouds before her face.

Casey opened his mouth to speak, then closed it again, completely stunned by her harsh tone. He and Taylor weren't exactly what you'd call best friends in elementary school, but he hadn't seen her in over five years. Wouldn't she have forgotten about that incident by now?

She sighed with exasperation, letting her heavy gear bag drop from her shoulder with a deep thud and tossing her stick across its top. Looking over both shoulders to make sure no one stood nearby in the bitter cold of the parking lot, she took two steps closer and lowered her voice so only Casey could hear. "Don't you get it? You were a liability. You threatened to blow my cover." Her hands balled into fists in a feeble attempt to contain her rising anger.

Casey blinked, scratching his wind-whipped hair with his numbing fingertips. "I don't know what you mean. What did I ever do to you?"

Taylor laughed one of those deep, cruel guffaws of disbelief that sliced deep into his heart. "It was *so* obvious, I thought you knew. Don't you remember back in Mrs. Shaw's fourth grade class when you spilled *blue* paint on my *white* jersey? It was so embarrassing to have to wear a pink Hello Kitty shirt from the lost and found for the rest of the day." She pushed him square in the chest, making him totter back a step onto his heels.

He straightened and placed a hand to his chest in a futile attempt to erase the spreading chill leftover from her touch. Giving her a slow nod, he remembered the only time he had ever seen her wear pink in all of their elementary years. "I'm really sorry about that. It was a total accident," he apologized, realizing his little mistake had obviously impacted her much worse than he originally thought.

"Oh, really," she replied, her tongue dripping with acid. She placed both hands on her hips and leaned menacingly forward. "And how about the time when you were right behind me at the drinking fountain, and the whole thing went wonky and suddenly drenched my face and hair?" The wind caught her black hair, making it flap behind her, intensifying the fury written across her face.

He willfully took a step backward, then shrugged. "It could've happened to anyone," he admitted.

"But it didn't!" she fumed, her words hitting him at the same time the wind's icy shards lashed Casey across the cheek. "You purposefully did those things to me. And I can't believe you were so naïve the whole time that you didn't even recognize the signs."

Casey dug his freezing hands deep into his pockets, regretting his choice of clothing; the long-sleeved shirt and jeans offered little reprieve from the frosty blast. He clamped his jaw shut to silence his chattering teeth and locked off his joints to halt his body's quivering long enough to think about what she had said. If Owen's statement was true, and he was really a water elly and Taylor an ice elly—even though a part of him couldn't even believe he entertained Owen's theory when he still didn't know how to describe that term—then maybe it *would* seem a little suspicious. Casey couldn't help that he had always felt somewhat awkward around Taylor from the first time he met her. He'd had a tendency toward clumsiness when he was young, not that he'd grown out of it altogether yet. That day in fourth grade, he'd simply tripped over his shoelace when he was walking down the aisle. The next thing he knew, the tray of blue paint had slipped out of his hands and splattered across the front of her home jersey for the Minnesota Wild. He distinctly remembered how quickly her mounting fury had replaced the initial look of shock.

Then it hit him. Blue paint for water on a white shirt for ice. And why else would the drinking fountain act "wonky," as she claimed, unless his awkwardness acted out through the water? Could that also explain the icy shards that had whipped across his face when her temper flared in the parking lot a few moments ago?

He smacked his hand against his forehead. The pieces were starting to fit together.

Meanwhile, Taylor continued her rant. "And then in fifth grade…remember when the mayor came to our school and presented you with an award in front of all of the students?"

Casey nodded, recalling the day the mayor—in front of the entire student body—treated him like a hero for saving his cousin over summer vacation. Pride had swelled in his chest as he stood with a broad smile in front of flashing cameras to accept the certificate of award.

A pride he felt Taylor was about to squelch.

The polar wind across the parking lot carried sharp crystals of ice that tore across his face, needle sharp. He suspected Taylor had exacerbated the conditions of the crisp night air to hammer home her point.

"That's when I realized you really didn't know," she said, a sharp edge to her tone. "I mean, seriously…how on earth could a ten-year-old possibly save his cousin from being dragged out to sea and drowning without *any* help? That didn't make you the least bit suspicious? But I figured, hey, maybe you really were clueless about the whole thing."

"Wow," Casey said in a wounded tone. "That stung a bit."

"Oh, stop," she said with a wave of her hand, like shooing away a pesky fly. "You know what I mean. Like I said before, *you* were a liability."

When she pointed directly at his chest, Casey felt another blast of icy air hit him straight on. The wind sliced through his hair, making his ears feel red and raw.

"Why do you think I open-enrolled at a different middle and high school than you?" she seethed. Her breaths came out heavy and fast, like anger boiled in her veins. "It wasn't just for the hockey program."

And all this time, Casey had thought hockey provided the sole reason she'd decided to go to Eastlake. To learn he, and he alone, had served as the impetus for her choice proved more than he could stand for one day. He blinked back a tear, shoving all his curiosity about ellies to the recesses of his mind. None of it mattered anymore, not when her rage against his actions as a naïve child stunned him, fracturing any remnant of their childhood friendship. Her biting words hurt in a way he had never imagined, chilling him deep into his soul and making his shoulders slump forward sadly. Maybe he should have listened to Lee's advice rather than ruin a past friendship over something he didn't understand.

The sharp wind pierced his outer layer, sending a shiver through his spine. He regretted not bothering to put on his hat and gloves in his attempt to race out the door after Taylor. Now he pulled his hat from his pocket and shoved it over his ears, realizing with dismay his efforts had come far too late to warm his body that felt like he'd fallen through thin ice and submerged under wintry lake water.

Forcing a large lump down his throat, he squeaked out

a feeble, "Sorry," and slowly turned to leave. He wondered if Owen had set her up to this, hoping to break down Casey to his most vulnerable state before their next race. If so, his efforts had worked. Owen had definitely won this round.

Though the wind died down as Casey trudged back across the icy parking lot, the air felt noticeably colder, like ice crystals hung on his every breath. He looked up at the bright twinkling specks of stars, astonishingly clear in the bitter night air. A white halo circled the moon, letting him know just how frigid it was tonight. He only saw moondogs when ice crystals suspended in the air bent the moonlight into a bright ring. Casey jammed his fingers deep into his pockets, kicking himself for leaving his jacket in the car. The glares he'd have received for wearing the navy and gold colors of the rival school seemed menial compared to Taylor's verbal attack tonight. He never realized how much he had inadvertently disrupted her life.

He let his head hang as he forced one frozen foot to plod in front of the other. In the background, he heard a car door slam shut and a distant beep of the lock engaging, but he didn't bother to turn around. With one heavy step after another, he crossed the slick parking lot, eager to drive home.

He only made it past a few rows of cars when he felt a tug on his jacket sleeve, spinning him around. He shuddered uncontrollably at the touch.

Taylor stood before him, some of the fury erased from her face, her pale blue eyes tinged with remorse. "Y'know, maybe that came out a little harsher than I meant it to."

Casey looked at her sideways. "Is that what you call an apology?"

"Hey, it's a try, isn't it?" Her lips softened into a small smile. "You caught me off guard, and I guess maybe I was a little too hard on you. But seriously, you really are just figuring this whole thing out now?" She threw a playful punch at his shoulder.

He blinked, stunned by the quick change in her demeanor.

He gave Taylor a wary nod, wondering where her thoughts led. Just a minute ago, she'd totally berated him for complete accidents that had happened years ago, and now she wanted to make amends?

"You look a little cold," she noticed. "Sorry about that. Why don't you grab your jacket and then," she leaned toward him and whispered directly in his ear, cupping her words with her glove to ensure her words reached him alone, "meet me by the back of the Zamboni doors." Her breath dusted his cheek with flecks of ice.

Casey backed away and stared at her, his blue eyes registering concern. "Are you sure?" he dared to ask.

"Sure, I'm sure." She let her grin grow wider.

"Okay," Casey agreed warily. He noticed a hint of warmth infusing his body, spreading from his frozen core through his limbs. Instant curiosity piqued inside him, overriding any skepticism he thought he should have about meeting her alone. If Owen had indeed put her up to this stunt, he must be really desperate to beat Casey the next time they met at the pool. Perhaps there was a chance Casey could turn this around in his favor, strengthening his mental toughness until he beat Owen at his own mind game.

He headed toward the car to grab his jacket, jamming his numb fingers into his gloves as he walked. Halfway there, he glanced over his shoulder, catching a glimpse of Taylor's carefree walk around the back of the building. Despite their recent lack of snow cover on the ground, the doors behind the arena held huge piles of white where the Zamboni emptied its load after resurfacing the rink's ice.

Had she really transferred to Eastlake just because of *him*? He shook his head with complete confusion, grabbed his jacket from the car, and hustled back to meet her, grateful to stuff his arms inside the sleeves as he walked. As he rounded the corner, a sudden blast of icy wind struck him, and he quickly zippered his jacket all the way. He turned his back to the wind, then heard its accompanying light laughter.

"Walk with me," Taylor said and waved him down a sidewalk leading away from the arena.

Casey quickly followed, finding it difficult to match her quick strides over the patches of ice littering the path. The bare tree branches cast sharp shadows from the streetlights overhead, giving the slight perception that a flurry of ice crystals trailed behind Taylor's brisk walk.

She didn't turn to acknowledge his presence until she reached a small frozen pond at the edge of the Eastlake High School property. She waved her hand again, motioning for Casey to follow.

"No one's ever crazy enough to come here at this time of the year," she explained.

"I can see why," Casey said as a shiver racked his spine. He removed one gloved hand from his pocket to zipper his jacket all the way to the top. As angry as she had grown at seeing him again, whatever she had to say to him now probably wouldn't take very long. "Do you come here often?" he wondered.

She shrugged. "It's a place to get away when I need a break. It's a lot of pressure to keep this hidden all the time. I try not to show anything during my games. I can't always control it, but I definitely don't want to make it obvious, if you know what I mean."

Casey didn't but nodded anyway.

Taylor continued. "When I was little, people always told me how great I was. Then I remember how I felt when I first learned, and I was sorry for you. My parents reassured me that I did have remarkable talent, but in the wake of that news, their words sounded hollow and empty. I spent the rest of my time on the ice, proving that I was good without any unusual abilities. I intentionally hid my powers, forcing myself to work even harder to reach my goals."

His eyebrows shot up to the top of his head. "Powers?" he asked, unable to contain his curiosity any longer.

She laughed, her mouth opening into a full grin. "I'm sure that doesn't surprise you as much as you think it does. Not after you got a taste of it just now in the parking lot."

He thought of the shards of ice caught in the wind and lashing across his cheeks. "I think I know what you mean."

The smile washed off her face. "Sometimes, I can't control it when I lose my temper."

"Because I asked you about ellies?" he wondered, turning to face her.

"What if there were college scouts in the stands?" she hissed and pushed Casey's chest away with frustration. "They could've heard you. You could've ruined everything. All of my opportunities for the future destroyed with one simple little word."

"If they even knew what that word meant," Casey noted. He took one of her hands in his to settle her emotions.

She pulled her hand free of his and continued walking down the path. "I'm not willing to take that chance. In fact, I shouldn't even be here. My parents told me it's dangerous and I have to keep it a secret. To never tell anyone. *Ever*." She released a heavy sigh. "And yet here I am with *you*, of all people." She spun toward him, pointing her finger directly at his face.

Casey swallowed hard. "That doesn't sound like much of a compliment."

She dismissed his attempt at sarcasm with a huff. "Don't you see? We're polar opposites. We're not meant to be together. It's better this way, not drawing attention to ourselves."

"Honestly, I just needed to know if this was real or if I was losing my mind," Casey spoke quickly to justify his actions. "So much has changed in my life in such a short time. I didn't know who to ask or who to trust. That's why I wanted to see you. I've known you forever, and…."

"And?" she prompted, crossing her arms over her chest. She shifted her weight to one side. The faint rays of moonlight turned her eyes a pale glacial blue that fixed on his face, waiting for him to finish.

"And...I trust you," he admitted. "I can't tell if Owen's only trying to get in my head or if he's actually trying to expose me to a whole new world I didn't know anything about."

"Who's Owen?" she asked, uncrossing her arms.

"Owen Teague? Oh, he's some new 'powerhouse' over at Great Plains," Casey said, using air quotes, trying to keep a casual tone despite the irritation bottled up inside him at the thought of Owen beating him by a fraction of a second. "He claims he's a fire elly, even though he's a swimmer. I still don't understand it fully."

Taylor shrugged. "Never heard of him."

Casey looked at Taylor with complete surprise. Either she was an impeccable liar, or she really didn't know the guy. Judging by the sincerity inscribed on her face, he assumed it was the latter. He'd known her forever, and despite what happened between them tonight, he sincerely trusted her; that was the primary reason he'd sought her out in the first place. Meaning, Owen really hadn't set her up to mess with Casey's head before their next race. That didn't erase all the anger she had directed at him earlier that evening, but it was a start.

They stood by the edge of the frozen pond in awkward silence for a while. The outside air no longer bothered Casey since he had other worries to consume him. Unanswered questions swam through his mind: if Taylor hadn't told anyone about her abilities, what signs did Owen use to recognize other ellies like her and Lee? Why did Owen believe Casey was a water elly when he didn't even know himself? And how did someone actually become an elly if such a thing truly existed in the real world?

Casey's brow crinkled with confusion. He felt grateful for a distraction from his bewildering thoughts when Taylor asked him, "Would you like me to show you something I can do with ice?"

"Definitely."

Taylor stripped the gloves off her hands and stowed them in her pocket. She bent down and cupped a handful of snow stuck in the tall grasses by the bank of the pond. Even though the snow was too cold and dry to pack, she placed it between her bare palms and somehow formed a hard, round snowball. Next, she flattened her fingers, pressing them firmly together. When she opened her hands, the snow had surprisingly crystallized into a solid block of transparent ice. Casey blinked, certain his eyes played tricks on him. He reached over and grabbed a handful of snow, mimicking her actions to replicate her results. He opened his hands. Just as he expected, he had no ice. Instead, the cold, dried flakes scattered between his fingers and dusted the ground, unable to stick together into a snowball.

Taylor hid her snicker behind one hand. Focusing her attention back to her block of ice, she continued her work without explanation. She squeezed the block of ice between her fingertips. Each time her fingers slid outward from the center, she fashioned the ice into a perfect flower petal. Taylor rotated the block in her hand until she had created a symmetrical flower with six curved petals. She held up her work for Casey to admire.

His mouth set into a smirk. "Don't get me wrong. That's absolutely amazing. But I dunno, it seems a little girly for you." All through grade school, Taylor had worn sporty T-shirts or hockey jerseys, except for the day he spilled paint on her, and she had to wear pink for lack of other options. And she'd already made it abundantly clear to him how she felt about the color pink.

"Funny," she said in a tone that didn't sound the least bit amused.

"What else can you do?" Casey asked, eager to ease the tension that seemed to build every time he spoke to her.

"Here's one of my favorites. But I'm only showing you

because I'm feeling a little better." She playfully bumped her shoulder into his. "You don't want to see me when I'm in a bad mood."

"I thought I already had," he said, remembering their exchange in the parking lot.

"Like I told you before, you just made me lose my temper. I wasn't in a bad mood," she clarified with a twisted smile.

"Oh, okay. I'll make a note of that." Casey rolled his eyes, hoping he never had to witness another one of her mood swings after tonight's rant against him.

Taylor leaned down to reach the surface of the pond, scraping her hand across the frozen water. She removed a thin layer of ice as easily as if she had shaved it off with a sharp tool.

She broke the piece into two nearly identical triangles, then touched them together at one point. Amazingly, they remained connected, like her body heat had briefly melted the ice before it refroze in that position.

Balancing the delicate triangles in her hand, Taylor blew softly across their surfaces, sending them to flight. The triangles floated in the breeze, gently flapping open and closed, resembling a translucent butterfly.

Speechless, Casey watched in awe.

The icy butterfly swooped in a wide circle overhead. It began its gradual descent, its wings flapping open and closed at regular intervals until it landed on the tip of Casey's nose.

Taylor chuckled.

Casey carefully plucked the ice wings off his nose to study, but the meager warmth from his hands radiating through his gloves somehow melted the connection instantly. "I didn't mean to ruin it," he apologized.

"It's no biggie," she said, her lips turning up in an amused yet satisfied grin. "Y'know, if you ever need someone to talk to, feel free to shoot me a text." She held out her hand expectantly.

It took Casey a minute to understand her intention. He

gave a belated response, "Oh. Sure," and fished his phone out of his pocket before she changed her mind. He unlocked the screen for her and passed her the phone. She took a quick selfie, wearing an uncharacteristically wide smile, and typed her number into his contacts list.

Her smile suddenly faded, and her eyes narrowed into thin slits. The rapid transformation in her disposition startled Casey.

"Just be discreet and don't ever spell out the whole word," she warned with a crisp, cool edge to her tone. "A lowercase 'e' will be enough for me to know what you mean."

She stood up to leave and briskly walked back down the illuminated trail, leaving Casey alone with his thoughts. A gust of arctic air hit him the second she was lost from view.

Suddenly, Casey smacked his glove against his forehead. How stupid could he be? Wrapped up in the display of her "powers," he had totally forgotten to ask her what the word "elly" actually meant. He raced after her, as fast as his feet would allow on the slippery trail, and rounded the corner of the arena. By the time he reached the parking lot, he spotted a pair of receding ruby taillights trailed by a cloud of exhaust, suspended like a thick white mass in the cold darkness. With a heavy sigh, he wondered if her abilities also allowed her to walk much faster over the icy ground. He had missed his opportunity to ask in person and knew he didn't dare bring it up over the phone.

Despite the barrage of unexplained questions that continued to flood his mind, he realized one thing for certain. He had learned a lesson when he didn't listen to Lee McCormick's advice. Judging by Taylor's icy glare and abrupt departure, Casey knew he'd better heed her warning.

CHAPTER SIX

Back at home, Casey dumped his backpack on his bedroom floor, grateful for the start of the weekend, so he didn't have to deal with his homework after everything he had experienced tonight. Even though his clock's angry red lights reminded him of the late hour, he knew what he must do to clear his mind so he could get a decent night's sleep. His evening with Taylor had provided more information than he could digest in one sitting—not just about the whole elly thing, but her unexpected sentiments toward him. Sadly, her phrase, "We're not meant to be together," echoed in his ears. She claimed she had transferred to Eastlake just to be away from him. Was he really that much of a liability? And if so, why hadn't she ever bothered to tell him before? Or why hadn't he seemed to notice the warning signs?

He set up the easel, then pulled a fresh canvas from his dwindling supply and started to recreate the image stuck in his head. He squeezed a huge glob of titanium white from the tube onto the palette and gradually tinted smaller dabs of lavender and light blue, letting them mix with the white. He dipped only the very tip of the bristles into a small cup of water, then let the brush flow across the canvas with bold, brash strokes at first to create a wash of color. Without waiting for the background to dry, he grabbed a smaller brush for fine detail work, adding boxy shapes and pairs of symmetrical triangles to the fresh paint to capture his mood. He painted with his face only inches from the canvas to better see the details of each precise brushstroke. Continually dipping into the paint on the palette, he repeated the shapes of cubes and triangles over and over again. Water thinned the shapes in the background while he kept the paint thicker for the ones in the foreground to create a perception of depth. He piled the outlines on top of one another until his fingers grew numb from the pressure of keeping his brush in the same position for so long.

"Better than being numb from the cold," he reminded himself. A residual shiver rattled his spine, reminiscent of the conditions he had endured during Taylor's tirade in the parking lot. He'd never seen her that irate before and hoped he would never cause her to feel that way toward him again.

His eyelids grew heavy as he put a few final touches on the painting, wanting to make sure the lines looked just as he'd remembered until he simply couldn't keep his eyes open any longer. Utterly exhausted, he washed the brushes and returned his paints to the toolbox, then crawled into bed without another glance at his work.

* * * *

Casey woke late the next morning, more focused and refreshed despite the dismal leaden sky that peeked through the windows, casting a dreary gray light and threatening imminent snow. Surprisingly, Taylor's initial outrage no longer fazed him. In fact, he had convinced himself the whole thing was just a bizarre dream. The blame, the apology, and the magic by the pond all made so much more sense as a concoction of his exhausted physical state compounding with the roller coaster track his mind had taken ever since Owen's comment after their one hundred backstroke race. It seemed the only logical way to explain something so far outside the realm of ordinary. He had invented the experience in his subconscious while he slept.

Remembering a way to check for certain, he stretched one hand out from under his warm covers and grabbed his phone off the nightstand. When he slid his finger across the screen to search his contact list, her phone number and picture were clearly visible. Casey gasped, so he hadn't made everything up, he thought, studying her photo on the screen. To him, her selfie almost seemed like a shimmer of ice crystals suspended in the dark, cold air around her, glistening like specks of diamond dust in the streetlights.

He set the phone back on the nightstand and pulled the covers up to his chin, trying to piece all of this together. If what she said was true, Taylor's abilities—or "powers," as she called them—changed his whole perception of the world. That would explain the pocket of warmth Casey had felt in the lane next to him, the brilliant colors of the sunset that streamed off Owen's form after every backstroke turn, and the orange hazy glow that encircled him as he exited the pool. Still, Casey had to admit doubt clouded his mind. Maybe they had something special about them, but he already knew a simple scientific explanation for his condition. The doctor said he had synesthesia, nothing else.

Casey sighed, wondering how he could clear his mind to focus on the next race with all of these confusing thoughts clogging his mind. He rolled over onto his other side, willing himself back to sleep when his gaze caught a rectangular flash of light colors across the room. He had completely forgotten about the finished painting on the easel and jerked upright, throwing off his covers. Rubbing the sleep from his eyes, he stared at the painting, his mouth agape.

The tints and blended colors resembled huge slabs of glacial ice, the same color as Taylor's piercing stare under the light of the moon. He had painted finer blocky crystals scattered across the foreground in a wispy trail like the impossibility she had fashioned in her hand, transforming a packed snowball into a large cube of transparent ice. Worse, the paired triangles that flittered up and down the borders resembled delicate butterfly wings in flight.

Casey swallowed hard. He contemplated pulling the covers back over his face and staying in bed the rest of the weekend to hide his embarrassment. Not only had he depicted ice...he had painted his impressions of *Taylor*, something, he quickly realized, she—and the rest of the world, for all he cared—could never know.

Acting fast, Casey leapt from his bed and crossed the room in three speedy steps. He removed the dried canvas from the easel, quickly stuffing it at the very bottom of the pile of paintings on his floor. Even though his mom would never make the connection between his work and a girl who had chosen to open enroll in another high school because of him, he wanted it far away from sight.

At a loss for words, Casey trudged down the stairs and entered the bright kitchen his mother had painted a sunny shade of yellow. She had reasoned the yellow reminded her of growing up in Florida, but Casey suspected otherwise. He figured she had selected the color to combat the dullness outdoors on days like this one. Usually, it worked, but today other thoughts burdened his mind.

As his mom prepared their special weekend breakfast together, the aroma of pancakes on the griddle filled his nose and provided a momentary distraction. His stomach responded with a delighted gurgle, making him remember he barely had anything for dinner before the game and had hadn't bothered to grab a bite after he got home, heading upstairs to paint the flurry of emotion trapped inside his memories instead.

Ellen Donnelly wiped her hands on the dishtowel, then

looked over her shoulder to wish him good morning. She dropped the spatula on the countertop with a clatter, her mouth falling agape. "Your face…it's as white as a ghost! Casey, what's wrong?"

Casey shrugged and slumped into a chair at the small wooden table, resting his palms on the table and letting his legs stretch as far as they could comfortably reach.

She crossed the floor in a few worried steps, then placed the back of her hand against his forehead, searching for a sign of fever. "Are you feeling all right?"

"I guess." He tried to muster a convincing smile, but it didn't really work.

She sighed, took a glance at the pancakes' progress as small bubbles began to rise through the circles of batter on the griddle, then pulled out the chair across from him. She set her elbows on the table and folded her hands together, letting her chin rest on top. "Remember what Coach Harris said after your last race?"

Casey nodded. "Something about needing a break."

"Honey, maybe this has all been too much for you," she added, her voice sweet as sugar. "Maybe you need a break. Just for the weekend. You always love going up to the lake."

"Mom, I'm in high school…I have three exams next week," he protested, thinking maybe he should have skipped the hockey game last night to get a head start on his mounds of work. "And if I drive up alone, you won't have a car for the whole weekend.

"So bring your homework with you and finish it up there. Grandma won't mind," she suggested, rising from her chair to flip the pancakes. "Besides, if I drive, you can get work done in the car. There's an extra two hours of studying for you." Her green eyes caught his, gauging his response.

Casey gave a noncommittal, "I dunno." He folded his hands together on the table and stared off into the distance at nothing in particular, trying to push away the image of the icy butterfly wings melting at his touch.

His mom joined him at the table again while the other side of the pancakes finished cooking. She placed a gentle hand over his that were folded with stress and gave a little squeeze. "Honestly, I think this will do you good. You have a lot on your plate right now. Sometimes, you just need to take a break and relax. I'm not asking you to miss school or swimming. And you don't have anything else on the schedule for this weekend. Besides, I have a heap of tests to grade, so I'll be a bore to be around. You won't be missing a thing."

Casey replied with a weighted sigh. His heavy eyelids fell into a sad, slow blink.

"Take a break, just overnight," his mom pressed. "It won't interfere with your training for Sections or your tapering for States. I think you really need a mental break to refocus. Don't you?"

"I guess," Casey said, though his tone remained neutral.

His mom smiled. "Great. Then I'll call Grandma and let her know." She gave a comforting squeeze on his shoulder, then stood up to take the pancakes off the griddle. A moment later, she placed a steaming pile on a plate in front of him, next to the butter and syrup.

Casey inhaled deeply. Maybe Mom was right, and he was overthinking this whole thing. As much as he wanted to convince himself his stomach wasn't ready to handle food just yet, the smell of warm breakfast quickly won him over. He forced his mind to go blank and accepted a bite of his food.

His mother smiled with satisfaction. She picked up her phone to make arrangements for the weekend.

Maybe everything would make more sense on a full stomach and a weekend away from the recent stressors in his life. One thing remained certain: Casey had better figure this whole confusing mess about ellies out soon. Otherwise, he could kiss his chances at State and the Olympics Trials goodbye.

CHAPTER SEVEN

Grandma Louise only lived an hour north, but Casey rarely visited her during the school year. Between his academics and athletic commitments, Casey's busy schedule usually left time for little else.

With a twinge of reluctance, Casey threw on a pair of sweats, packed an overnight bag, stowed his hat and gloves inside the zippered pockets of his jacket, and stuffed his backpack full of his homework assignments. He habitually grabbed his latest paintings to show her, then reconsidered. How could he explain the streak of wildfire raging through the middle of the canvas or the flurry of icy butterfly wings in flight? He needed more time to contemplate the meanings behind those works.

Ellen offered to drive him up north so he could work on his homework during the ride. He waited until they reached the highway to pull out his math textbook and problem set, but before he could start on the first problem, she asked, "Are you sure you're okay? You seem unusually quiet this morning."

Casey closed his problem set inside the book and shifted his eyes out the window as the bare tree branches blurred into a single shade of dull brown. How could he elaborate without revealing too much information? He decided to heed Taylor's warning and stick with a vague reply. "I guess I've just got a lot on my mind."

His mom shot him a quick glance. "You know, it was only one race, and it's not even your best stroke," she said in an understanding voice. "It doesn't change anything. I know you had the perfect season going into that event, but winning isn't everything. Maybe Coach Harris wanted to find a new way to challenge you and help you grow before going into Sections."

Somehow that didn't make him feel much better. Though it would have been a remarkable achievement, it wasn't like he had to finish his entire regular season undefeated. And maybe he would have if he didn't let Owen prove such a distraction before the race had even begun.

When he didn't reply, she continued her pep talk. "You'll get another chance. I know you will. Besides, you haven't shaved or started your taper yet. There's plenty of room for improvement." He could hear the sugar coating on each word.

He knew she was just trying to make him feel better, but she didn't understand that it wasn't the outcome of the race that bothered him this much. He opened his mouth to explain, then reconsidered. "It's not that."

"If not the two one-hundredths of a second, then what?" she asked. She pulled her eyes from the road for a second longer this time, and he could see the lines of concern and worry creasing her face.

Casey's mind drifted to his memories of the unexplained heat radiating from Owen Teague's handshake. He remembered how the water around Owen's lane changed color, flowing and swirling in bright shades of orange and red, and how Owen himself seemed to glow even out of the water.

After his mom's stunned reaction years ago on the North Carolina beach, Casey knew better than to try to explain these visions to her. Her shocked expression at his mention of unnatural colors in the ocean proved warning enough that his perceptions existed outside the realm of ordinary. So he attempted to close the conversation with a general, "It's not a big deal. You wouldn't understand." He let his gaze shift out the window, hoping his answer would suffice for now.

A few minutes passed in silence before his mom dared to ask, "Is it about the girl?"

"Who?" Casey glanced back at his mom, uncertain of the direction of her new angle.

She shrugged but kept her eyes focused on the road. "The one from the school paper," she clarified.

"Mandi?" Casey nearly snorted at the sound of her name. Sure, her stunning appearance and vivacious personality had initially appealed to him, but it didn't take long to see another side of her character. He eventually realized Mandi was more interested in his accomplishments than in Casey himself. Especially when she had quickly turned her attention toward Owen, practically flirting with him by the side of the pool. She wouldn't have even bothered to talk to him if Casey hadn't been the one to beg her to find out information for him, he reminded himself, but there was nothing he could do about it now. He had needed answers at the time and had no other choice. Still, it wasn't fair of him to blame her for liking Owen's confident, albeit sometimes arrogant, demeanor. "No, it's definitely not her," he said.

The creases of worry on her face softened a bit. "She didn't seem your type anyway."

Casey let his head sink into the headrest, wondering what kind of girl his mom thought was his type. Someone sporty like Taylor, perhaps? Then again, Casey hadn't even begun to understand Taylor's rapid changes in her temperament. One minute she detested him, pushing him in the chest with her hard, cold touch, and the next, she playfully joked with him, slugging his shoulder in jest. Plus, Taylor did claim they were polar opposites. Casey found it nearly impossible to recover from a comment like that.

He opened his math text again as a subtle hint and attempted to work through the next few problems, though his efforts proved fruitless. No matter how many times he read through the word problem, none of the information made any sense in his muddled mind. His thoughts continually drifted between the sensations in the pool before his race against Owen, the casual half-court shot Lee blindly sunk behind his back, and the flower and butterfly Taylor fashioned from ice down at the frozen pond. None of it made any sense. And he felt afraid to tell others that he could read the water? Reading the water was nothing compared to Taylor's floating butterfly that melted in his hand. Their abilities opened a whole new door on the realm of extraordinary talent.

He began to regret agreeing to visit Grandma Louise this morning; this whole weekend getaway felt like a waste of his time. Why did his mom think getting away from his normal routine would actually help in this scenario? He couldn't focus on his work. The commute north burned away a precious hour of his limited weekend and would force him to rush through the rest of his assignments to make Monday's deadlines.

By the time they turned off the highway, he had only made it through half the problem set and doubted any of his answers were correct. Casey packed his homework away, knowing from past experience the winding country roads made his stomach uneasy, twisting and churning as the car bounced over the narrow and uneven asphalt. He feigned sleep for the last ten minutes of the trip to avoid another uncomfortable conversation, pulling his hood up over his head to buffer the cold and letting it lean against the window. There wasn't much to see at this time of year anyway. Beneath a drab heavy sky, dull sticklike trees stretched toward the nonexistent sun. A fine layer of snow coated their bare branches, leftover from the last passing storm. A few tall evergreens provided the only splash of color on this bleak day. At least the thick gray clouds hadn't yet spilled their contents and slowed their travel. He expected his mom would make it back home before the first flakes began to fall.

Each summer, Casey loved coming up here a few weekends when the afternoon sun glimmered off the water. He remembered how his mouth filled with the taste of juicy mouthfuls of soft-skinned peaches and a tall glass of strawberry lemonade every time he visited the lake. He'd take out the canoe and paddle past the neighbor's waterfronts, bathed in purple flowering hostas and bright orange daylilies. He'd listen to the familiar hum of a boat engine towing a water skier in a huge loop and the wake repeatedly lapping against the side of his canoe after they passed. The warm weather teemed with life: the lakeside echoed with the chorus of chirping crickets and croaking frogs, while the treetops filled with cheerful songbirds and chattering squirrels. Sometimes he even spotted the bright white head and tail feathers of a bald eagle soaring overhead in search of a tasty meal.

Together, he and Grandma Louise would sit outside in the evenings beneath overflowing baskets of fuchsia flowers hanging along the back deck. As the dusk faded into night, they'd count fireflies in the cool night air until the voracious mosquitoes forced them indoors.

But today, the whole area looked bleak and barren in uniform shades, representing gray skies and white expanses of frozen ponds and lakes with much more snow cover along the side of the road than they had back home. Taylor's comment about "polar opposites" again leapt into his head, visualizing the stark differences in colors from one season to the next. He drew his attention away from the frozen water and stared blankly at the colorless sky for the remainder of the trip.

A ways down the road, his mother took a sharp right turn onto a long and narrow gravel driveway that wound through deep snowbanks and ended in front of a cream-colored rambler with a slate gray roof and detached garage. The sight of Grandma Louise's house, even on this bleak and barren day, elicited warm memories of summers on the water. The ice cover, usually over a foot thick this time of year, subdued the taste of fresh peaches and a tall glass of lemonade in his mouth, making it seem more like he scooped big spoonfuls of peach ice cream and lemon sorbet instead. Ellen stopped in front of Grandma Louise's porch, covered in thick piles of white along the railings and Adirondack chairs, and turned off the car, leaving the keys resting halfway in the ignition. Casey barely had time to climb out with his armfuls of belongings before a golden retriever sprang through the front door of the house and bounded up to greet him. His tail wagged with so much joy, it slammed repeatedly into Casey's knees.

"How's it going, Bo?" Casey asked, surprisingly feeling his spirits lift already. He shuffled his bags and jacket to his left arm so he could bend down and scratch the dog behind the ear with his free hand. Bo's hindquarters dropped into a sitting position by Casey's side. The dog's mouth gaped open into what appeared a most satisfied toothy grin. Once Casey found just the right spot to scratch on the back of his neck, Bo's hind leg thumped the ground with delight. Casey couldn't help but smile in return.

Without warning, Bo leapt to his feet and scampered through the deep snow, covering the yard with happy, lighthearted bounces. Though most golden retrievers Casey had seen in his neighborhood kept their tails down when they went for walks, Bo held his high in the air like a startled white-tailed deer.

Dressed in a knitted sweater beneath her tan fleece jacket, wooly lined boots that covered her pants up to her knees, and a thick burgundy hat sitting on top of the silver curls that framed her face, Grandma Louise walked over to the car to give Casey and Ellen warm hugs. "Would you like to come in for a bit?"

she offered her grayish-blue eyes, the color of the sky at twilight, twinkling with anticipation.

Ellen shook her head. "No, I'm good," she said. "Casey and I talked the whole way up."

Casey blinked, startled by her reply. He felt like he had deliberately evaded all of her questions.

"Not even for a cup of coffee?" Grandma Louise suggested with a welcoming gesture of her gloved hand toward the front door.

His mom forced her lips into a warm smile. "I really should be getting back. Lots of tests to grade," she said, covering her emotions with a false attempt of a joyful tone.

Grandma Louise leaned closer and whispered something too low for Casey to hear. He studied his mom's reaction; her eyes seemed glassy, on the verge of tears. Still, she managed to remain composed in front of him. Casey wondered if he had upset her too much, making her worry that his silence signaled something worse: a sign they had started to drift apart.

Grandma Louise warmly wrapped her arms around Ellen again. "Everything will be okay," she said in a voice loud enough for Casey to hear this time. "I promise."

Casey waved to his mom as she backed out of the driveway, wishing he could say something to make up for his silence during the trip, wishing her pale green eyes spoke forgiveness and understanding rather than sadness and confusion. Only how could he explain something he didn't yet understand himself?

"So, how have you been, Casey," Grandma Louise asked, placing a gentle hand against his back.

He shrugged, letting his eyes fall to his feet. "Pretty good."

"No new paintings to show me today," she asked, surveying his load.

"Nah. I haven't had the time to whip out the paints." He hoped his response sounded convincing.

"I see," she said, regarding him with skepticism. "Well,

come on in. It's always nice of you to stop by." She held open the front door for Bo, who bounded in out of the snow and proudly strutted in front of Casey, bouncing on his heels with each step.

He carried his jacket and bags inside and looked around. Grandma Louise's modest house hadn't changed in years. Hand-carved duck decoys decorated her walnut coffee and end tables, reminding him of his grandpa's favorite hobby before he had passed away years before. Vibrant knitted afghans lay over the backs of chairs and couches, a grandfather clock loudly ticked away each passing second, and a sweeping bay window overlooking the lake commanded his attention, even on a day like today when there wasn't much variety of color outside. Bo quickly found his favorite spot to curl up on a fluffy area rug in the middle of the wooden floor panels. Casey knelt down next to him and scratched behind his ear, finding the simple action simmered his frustration leftover from the drive, letting his body melt into a relaxed state. He only planned to stay overnight. Somehow he'd find a way to get everything done.

He glanced around the family room, spotting several of his abstract paintings hanging in wooden frames against the dated floral wallpaper, evident of his change in his style over the years. He peered more closely at his work, envisioning a jump off the dock into the lake with his eyes wide open, moonlight shimmering off glassy water like a flashlight beam piercing the indigo night, and concentric circles of his canoe paddle dipped in the water on a fishing trip with his grandpa. To anyone else, the unusual combination of colors and lines would appear abstract in nature, but to Casey, the bold greens resembling the colors of Granny Smith apples, kiwis, and honeydew melon, and stark brushstrokes helped him relive favorite memories of summers past. Long ago, he'd noticed his grandma couldn't ever part with a gift from her only grandchild. "No matter how bad it looks," Casey muttered and crinkled his nose at one of his earliest pieces, cringing at its numerous flaws.

"Make yourself at home," Grandma Louise said, bringing out a plate of fresh baked oatmeal raisin cookies. "Lunch will be ready soon." She returned to the kitchen.

Casey nodded and left Bo to deposit his bags down on the floor of the guest room. A single bed covered in flannel sheets and a hand-sewn quilt sat along one wall, opposite a futon couch that could open into a second bed if needed. Lacy curtains muted the scant rays of gray light through the single window. He tossed his jacket on the futon and started to unpack, stacking his books one by one on the nightstand when his grandma called from the kitchen, "I know your mom said you have a bunch of homework this weekend. But before you begin, I'd like you to tell me what you saw."

Casey blinked with confusion. He dumped the rest of his books on the guest bed and stuck his head out the door. "Huh?"

"At your last race," she clarified, her voice carrying down the hall.

How could she possibly know about that? Is that what his mom had told her in their hushed conversation in the driveway before she drove back home?

Casey left everything in the guest room and joined her in the kitchen. He grabbed two glasses from the cabinet and filled each with milk before setting them down for lunch. "I don't really know what you're talking about."

"Casey," she coaxed him, putting a gentle, wrinkled hand on Casey's arm, "try me."

"You won't believe me," he said with an exaggerated sigh and sunk into a chair at the kitchen table. After a few moments of silence, he confessed his initial observations about how he read the water differently in his last race but decided to omit the parts about Lee and Taylor. No one would believe such outlandish tales.

Grandma Louise gave Casey a sympathetic smile. She confessed in a melancholy voice, "I had hoped you'd never find out." She set two plates and two sets of silverware on the kitchen table next to the plate of cookies. She had already laid out a loaf of bread and an assortment of meat and cheese, lettuce, tomato slices, and condiments in her version of a build-your-own-sandwich bar.

Suddenly Casey didn't feel hungry. His stomach flipped with worry. "Never find out what?" A million questions flew to the front of his mind, vying for his attention, desperate for him to voice each one. Yet Casey silenced them all, exhausting his patience as he prayed she would elaborate.

Grandma Louise joined him at the table. She clasped her hands together in her lap. "I really didn't want it to destroy your life like it did your father's." A weighted sigh slowly escaped her lips. "I made a mistake with him," she explained, her wrinkled mouth sagging into a deep frown. "I told him the truth right before you were born, just in case there was a chance he had passed it along to you. But it was my mistake." She shook her head sadly, her eyes filled with regret. "He didn't handle the news well. He felt ostracized and alone, especially during such a pivotal time when he was starting a family. Instead of embracing the news and finding a way to incorporate it into his life, he shunned every aspect of his past and essentially disappeared." Her gaze left Casey's face and focused instead on fixing herself a turkey and cheese sandwich.

Casey blinked in disbelief. No one had ever shared this story before, even in this fragmented form. Hearing her words only raised more unanswered questions. He opened his mouth to speak, but his grandma wagged a finger at him to wait while she continued her tale.

"I was so glad when your mother brought you to the doctor, and you were diagnosed with synesthesia. It was perfect," she added, her steel-blue eyes sparkling with delight. "People aren't ready to know about us. They're not capable of comprehending it, so it's easier to mask behind something with a natural, scientific explanation. The fusion of senses, isn't that right?"

Casey nodded robotically, his mind churning wildly as he processed her every word. If it wasn't synesthesia, then what in the world was his grandma talking about?

"Please, Grandma. Stop right there," he spoke quickly, unable to contain the mounting questions any longer. "You keep talking about 'it,' but to be honest, I have no idea what 'it' actually is. What exactly are you saying? What's wrong with me?" He perched on the edge of his chair, desperate for answers.

"Nothing, dear. Absolutely nothing is wrong with you," she assured him. "Except for the fact that you're not eating. Since when is a teenage boy not hungry?"

"Sorry," Casey said and began to stack ham, cheese, and a tomato slice on a piece of bread. He added a light stroke of mustard to the top and forced a bite to appease her. He took a hard swallow, letting his mind chew through his thoughts. "Okay, then," he finally said, struggling to keep an even tone. "How am I different from everyone else? Are you saying it's something besides my synesthesia?" He made himself take another bite of his sandwich, chewing mechanically. The bread lodged in his throat, impossible to swallow. He drank a large gulp of milk to help wash it down.

At the sound of clinking silverware, Bo awoke and joined them in the kitchen. He stood next to the table, eyeing the lunchmeats with delight. "Let's get you outside," Grandma Louise told Bo and opened the front door to let the dog romp around in the snow, away from the food. She returned to her spot and resumed the conversation. "Of course it's not," she said, shaking her head with resolution.

He'd spent the last six years believing the doctor's diagnosis, the only logical explanation for his ability to read the water. That was how he saw the rip current and saved his cousin Jason. And that was how he managed to perform so well in his meets, giving him an advantage over his competition. And now she was saying it wasn't synesthesia all this time? How could she possibly know that? She wasn't a doctor.

Still, something about her mannerisms exuded confidence…a confidence Casey had trouble denying.

"Then what do I have?" he dared, his sandwich poised in front of his mouth, though he couldn't manage to take another bite at the moment, not when his stomach rolled inside, filled with uncertainty.

"Oh, Casey, don't make it sound like it's some awful disease," she chuckled, dismissing his worry with a flick of her wrist. "It's purely hereditary and has been in our family for thousands of years."

Casey tugged on his hair with frustration. She still hadn't said what "it" was! "What on earth are you talking about?"

"Finish your lunch, and I'll show you in the basement," she instructed as they heard a scratching noise at the front door. She left the table again to let Bo inside.

Casey shoved a few more bites of sandwich into his mouth, his jaw moving at a rapid pace as he tried to figure out what secrets lay in the basement. But the food, even her famous homemade cookies, held little taste, his mind too preoccupied with what she planned to show him. Stuffing the last bit of food into his cheek, he cleaned his spot and put the dishes in the sink, chewing while he worked.

Satisfied, she beckoned to him. "Come right over here," his grandma said on her way down the stairs. She led him to the small bookshelf next to the wood fireplace.

Grandma Louise pulled an old book off the shelf and cracked open its weathered spine. After sitting in her humid basement for the past few decades, its pages were brittle and yellowed with age.

"But Grandma," Casey objected, "this is a children's book. You've already read it to me about a hundred times."

She gave him a knowing wink. "Only when you were little,

you didn't know how to read between the lines," she corrected him and situated herself on the couch, tossing an afghan blanket over her legs and turning on the lamp on the end table beside her.

Casey felt simultaneously confused and curious. He took a tentative seat next to her on the couch, scrunching his nose at the musty smell of the old hardbound book. Within seconds, Bo leapt up alongside him, spun three tight circles in a row, and plopped down with his heavy head in Casey's lap. The dog soon occupied more than half the couch, leaving Casey and his grandma squished into the other half. Bo dropped into a fast slumber, bringing a smile to Casey's lips as he gently stroked the dog's golden fur as he returned his attention to the book.

The title, *Ancient Engineering Marvels*, filled more than half the page in a simple, outdated font. She cracked open the cover and turned to the first page. The illustration depicted an opulent city, an island set like a solitary gem in the middle of a sapphire sea. Canals encircled the island like concentric circles, with a single road bridging the mainland with the island's center. A tall peak stood alone in the heart of the island, its summit capped with a monumental Greek temple of sparkling white stone pillars that supported a great roof of glittering gold. Casey quickly scanned the caption describing how Atlantean citizens used advanced technologies for transportation and metallurgy.

Meanwhile, Bo's restless paws began to twitch as he rapidly entered his dreamlike trance. Soon, his legs swept into a pseudo-running motion, making Casey suspect the dog imagined himself chasing squirrels across the yard.

He chuckled before returning his focus to the illustration. "So that's Atlantis?" he asked, recognizing the concentric rings around the center of the city surrounded by water. "What does that lost civilization have to do with my synesthesia?"

Grandma Louise turned to him, her lips curling up into a knowing grin. "Why, dear, can't you see? You don't have synesthesia at all." Her grayish-blue eyes, creased with age, held his expectantly.

How would she know the doctors had misdiagnosed him? Casey stopped petting Bo for a moment and gave her a blank stare, looking from her face to the book and back again, more confused than ever.

When he didn't respond in words, she finished for him. "You are an elemental."

CHAPTER EIGHT

"An elemental? What's that?" Casey asked. The words rolled slowly off his lips as if saying them faster would make the concept seem more real.

She clarified, "Well, a *water* elemental, to be exact. It means that you can embody the powers of nature, specifically those powers that deal with water."

A water *elemental*? She must be out of her mind. He had to stop letting all this talk of the paranormal get under his skin. Sure, Owen managed to turn the water warm around him when he swam in the lane next to Casey. And Taylor said she possessed certain abilities or powers as well. Granted, she was able to turn snow into ice and make it flutter on the wind, but it wasn't like she was some type of superhuman being. She was simply Taylor, someone he'd known his whole life.

But seriously…*elementals*? How ridiculous of an idea was that? Like people could actually control elements in their favor. Like *Casey* knew how to control the water. "Oh, please," he muttered under his breath.

Grandma Louise began reading from the book. "The

classical Greek philosopher, Plato, described the lost city of Atlantis and its defeat by the Athenians, but many didn't and still don't believe his tale, dismissing it entirely as a work of fiction. Little do people realize this sunken city represents an early clash between the earth elementals and the water elementals. Today we live in peace together, but back then, the division had scaled into a full-blown battle."

"I take it, water won," Casey noted, vaguely recalling the end of the legendary story. "But here it says Atlantis was swallowed up by the ocean in one night and a day. No one knows where it's found. Even though divers have searched for evidence of the lost city, everything about its existence still remains a mystery. So how do you know the story is even true?"

"That's why you need to read between the lines," she pointed at him, her eyes flashing with excitement.

"So you're saying I need to visualize a world where earth and water elementals influenced the forces of nature?"

"Yes," she encouraged him and held the book closer to him, careful to avoid bumping into Bo's large head, still dozing on Casey's lap.

Casey thought for a minute, searching for a logical cause for such a monumental disaster. "Maybe the whole city sunk when a volcanic eruption generated a tsunami. I remember learning about that possibility when we studied plate tectonics in my earth science class last year."

"That's a good start. Now, imagine the volcano and tsunami didn't begin from forces within the earth," she prompted.

Casey's jaw dropped. "You're saying a *person* could create an eruption? Or a powerful wave that could destroy an entire civilization?"

She waved her index finger back and forth, amending his response. "Not just any person, dear. An elemental. Working together, the elementals could generate considerable force, enough to trigger events that normal people would consider natural disasters, like volcanic eruptions, earthquakes, and even massive tsunamis."

Casey shook his head, the color draining from his face. "Y'know, I find this really hard to believe. In school, they told us—"

"A different explanation," Grandma Louise nodded, finishing his sentence for him. Her lips turned up into a small smile. "An explanation that has been crafted for millennia to protect the secrets of the elementals."

Casey thought about her words for a long moment in silence. He envisioned the grand city of Atlantis sinking beneath the rising waters, not from a cataclysmic force of nature but from the powers residing inside of someone.

Someone like him.

He gave a low whistle, letting her words finally sink in. "It's crazy that they could possess that much control and that much destruction. And scary." He shuddered at the thought.

"Indeed," she agreed with a nod. "Like I said, today they fortunately live in peace, so we don't experience events of that magnitude. Nowadays, you have to search much harder for evidence of our existence. The ruins of Atlantis are perhaps one of the most famous examples of the destructive power of elementals. But the elementals more often used their powers for the good of the people around them. Let me show you a few other examples from the past so you can better understand."

Grandma Louise flipped ahead a few pages and read, "The ancient Polynesians sailed double-hulled canoes on long voyages, often covering thousands of miles across the vast Pacific. Using the prevailing winds from the southeast, they successfully sailed to and colonized all the thousand islands in the South Pacific, and even reached the coast of the Americas long before the Vikings and Christopher Columbus sailed to the New World."

"But there's nothing to read between the lines this time, Grandma," Casey objected. "This has nothing to do with elementals. You know Mom loves talking about the history of exploration – it's one of her favorite units – and she told me the Polynesians were amazing navigators. She said they used the stars, the waves, clouds, and birds to help them reach distant islands, even when they left the familiar stars in the Southern sky and sailed north to discover the Hawaiian Islands."

She nodded. "True, they were exceptionally skilled at navigating the Pacific, but the air elementals aided them by filling their sails with wind. The water elementals brought favorable currents their way, carrying their boats to distant lands."

"Are you sure?" he contested. "Because I thought you just read they used the prevailing winds from the southeast."

"But when those failed…." She paused, waiting for him to connect the pieces together like when he'd find all the straight edges to complete the border on a jigsaw puzzle before filling in the middle.

"Then I thought they brought out the paddles," Casey continued. He'd heard this story at almost the same time every year when his mom reached that topic with her students. "The Polynesians were skilled at paddling their outrigger canoes. Mom showed me pictures of their war canoes and told me people still celebrate their heritage today by racing outriggers for sport."

"Ah, but the ancient Polynesians possessed great reverence for the air and water elementals and for their assistance in exploring the Pacific Ocean," Grandma Louise noted, finishing the unwritten portion of history.

She flipped to another page where knights in armor bore long, decorative swords. Each knight had a large red cross emblazoned across his chest shield. "In the Middle Ages, the fire elementals helped craft great weapons for the Crusades," Grandma Louise read. "Working long hours in the forges, they designed and produced more than simple crude weapons. Their craftsmanship and expertise forged magnificent blades for the Crusader knights, conferring status and nobility to the bearer of the weapon."

He whipped his face toward hers, his brow furrowed. "Are you certain they just weren't really good bladesmiths?" he countered.

"I'm positive. No one else could withstand the exposure to the heat of the forge for such a long duration of time unless they had special abilities."

Casey stroked Bo's soft fur across his forehead, not entirely convinced. "So you're saying that fire and heat don't affect them as much as normal people."

She smiled. "Now you've got it. Here, let me show you one more." She turned back a couple of pages in the book. Three pyramids towered above the desert landscape.

"Those are the Pyramids of Giza." Casey recognized the distinctive shape from his mom's unit on the ancient Egyptians. Inside, each tomb held the remains of a mummified Egyptian pharaoh.

"The pharaohs appointed officials to oversee the massive workforces required to construct these monuments. These took thousands of workers over twenty years to build as they hauled the large blocks up ramps using ropes and sleds."

Casey scratched his head. "But I thought slaves built the pyramids."

"*Earth* elemental slaves specifically chosen for their abilities to cut and move such massive stones," she clarified.

"I don't get it. If they had special powers, wouldn't others have recognized that and treated them as gods like the other elementals?"

"Unfortunately, you cannot control who your parents are. Many were born into slavery and remained there. In those days, it wasn't easy to change your destiny. So the appointed officials specifically sought those with special powers and used them to help with the construction of the pyramids."

"I dunno," Casey said, and sank back into the couch,

crossing his arms over his chest. "I'm not buying it. Do you really expect me to think that all of the history I learned in school was fake?"

"Not fake, just an alternate explanation of the truth," she explained.

This was a lot to digest all at once. He began petting Bo again, hoping the repetitive motion would help settle his mind. "Go on," he dared, bracing himself for the rest.

"In ancient times, historians recorded their stories onto papyrus, wax boards, or scrolls. Later, monks painstakingly transferred these written works by hand. Throughout human civilization, those in power have dictated which works survived and which ones were destroyed. When powerful individuals thought differently and disregarded these works, they often ordered the books to be burned in order to gain control of the flow of information. All too often, entire libraries and royal collections were consumed in flames. Sometimes, a few copies of certain works survived."

"And other times, all that information was lost forever," Casey added.

"Exactly." Grandma Louise sighed. "Unfortunately, this practice continues today as radical militants destroy religious and historical artifacts, many of which are still documented in original handwritten pages. Historians work to preserve these endangered manuscripts, photographing them page by page for future generations to better understand the past."

"Mom's told me some of those stories before," Casey recalled. "I just didn't realize it was still happening."

"Sad, isn't it?" she said, silently flipping through a few other pages as if lost in her own thoughts.

Casey nodded, letting the pieces of the puzzle settle into place. Grandma Louise had just said that during ancient times, those in power controlled the flow of information and what records remained for others to study. His mother had talked to him about the role of a historian to take into consideration the impact of bias in historical accounts. Only, he never expected that lesson to hit so close to home. "Is that why this story hasn't been told before?" he asked.

"Yes." She paused on another page, looking up for a moment from the book. "Many of our kind have worked to keep the truth concealed."

"So, I guess you're going to tell me that elementals helped construct other marvels, like the Great Wall of China?" he guessed.

She flashed him a wide grin. "Now you're catching on. These feats and remarkable advancements would have been nearly impossible to accomplish had it not been for the assistance of the elementals of that time period. Still, some sought greater recognition and wanted to have their people worship them as gods.

"In ancient times, elementals could push their powers to the limit and were revered as gods. Priests in ancient Mexico and Central America were often elementals. They could block out the sun or withhold the rain to increase tributes to their gods, thereby encouraging greater piety and homage to the deities of the Mayan and Aztec civilizations. Today, fewer societies practice polytheism. As a result, elementals need to be more discreet with powers to avoid detection.

"It's not really any different now," she continued. "Admiring fans respect, even worship, professional athletes today. Some elementals use their talents to reach the pinnacle of their professional sporting careers. Surrounded by media hype and paparazzi, multi-million dollar athletes' lifestyles are not much different than those elementals of the past, heralded as heroes amongst their civilizations. We often treat sports stars the same way. We push them to continually impress us with more and more fantastically impossible feats until their personal signatures alone are worth a small fortune."

As Casey listened, his mouth fell open. This sounded almost like the same thing Owen had talked about, hinting that other athletes were ellies like him.

"Unfortunately, wealth and fame don't suit them all. Some thrive in that environment, while others can't handle the pressure or the temptations that arise due to their massive popularity." Grandma Louise gave him a small, sad smile.

"It's like the elementals of the past: we treat them as gods for their amazing abilities and talents, thereby forbidding them to lead a normal, happy life?" Casey concluded.

"Yes, only no one has to know," his grandma reminded him. "The general public doesn't understand our powers since they lie outside the natural explanations of the physical world."

Bo interrupted her story with a sudden sleep jerk. He groggily lifted his head from Casey's lap, found his way to his feet, and dropped onto the floor to stretch. His back bent into a deep arch, then he curled up at Casey's feet and drifted back to sleep within seconds.

Grandma Louise shook her head with amusement. "The carefree life of a dog. Sorry for the interruption. So where were we?"

"You said something about the public not understanding," he reminded her.

"Ah, yes." She nodded, remembering her train of thought. "Mind you, these are guarded secrets which would threaten the fabric of our society if revealed," she cautioned. A small part of her warning reminded Casey of the same fear Taylor exhibited down by the pond.

"I don't think I told you, but Owen called me a 'water elly' after our race. I thought it was just a joke, like a play of words on my last name," he said.

"I have to admit I haven't heard that one before, but you know how kids are these days. Your connection with nature fades, replaced instead with close ties to technology. Everything's shortened like you're always in a rush and don't have time to even speak the whole word. Your generation is always texting, always on a device. Why, I wouldn't be surprised if cursive, and all handwriting for that matter, soon becomes obsolete with your voice recognition software. No, it doesn't surprise me one bit if the elementals came up with a nickname for our kind."

Casey rubbed Bo's soft fur for comfort, letting his mind digest this implausible, alternate version of history. He had to admit, it was hard to undo the years of studying for his social studies classes in an instant of learning new information. "But Grandma, something doesn't make sense. I don't have any of the powers you described. If I was truly a water elemental, wouldn't I be able to affect the rain and the seas? Wouldn't I have the power to bend a stream of water or change its direction and force? I've never had the ability to do any of these things. The weather doesn't mirror my moods; it doesn't suddenly start to rain whenever I'm feeling blue. And I can't create a giant wave in the ocean or hold my breath for more than one length of the pool. How do you even know I'm an elemental at all?"

Grandma Louise smiled. "I believe the ability manifests itself differently in each person. You were granted the talent to read the water." She gestured to his paintings that lined the walls of her basement.

Casey's brow knitted. "You knew? This whole time, you knew what I had painted?"

She nodded. "Why did you think I always asked for some of your recent works? Besides the fact you are my only grandchild."

"I thought Mom told you they were just abstract, and they didn't have any meaning."

"Maybe she claims to view them that way so you don't think she worries about how you see the water," Grandma Louise proposed.

"So you saying she's known all this time?" Casey asked in

a defeated tone.

"Of course, she doesn't know the real reason you can read the water, but I suspect she thinks you've been holding some things back ever since the day you saw the water turn red, defining the rip current. I think she notices a connection between the times you choose to paint and how closely they follow the time you've spent in the water. The diagnosis of synesthesia provides the perfect cover, however, but it's still hard for her to understand why you would experience multiple, unrelated senses, for instance, every time you read a book or go for a swim."

A twinge of guilt filled Casey's heart. This whole time he'd kept his feelings hidden to prevent his mother's concern. And now, he realized his concealment had only augmented her worry, making her feel like he was intentionally keeping secrets from her. But how could he keep a secret when he hadn't even known the real reason? "I couldn't see the colors in the water before that day at the beach. Why do you think everything suddenly changed?" he wondered.

"Fear is a powerful motivator," his grandmother said. "You first unlocked your senses in desperation to save your cousin. Later, you learned how to channel that energy toward your swimming career. You've possessed this power your whole life, only you never needed to use it in the past. Now you need to…if you want to win, that is."

Casey let a heavy sigh escape his lips before he dared to speak again. "So you're saying these people — these *elementals* — live among us? Right here in society? And no one really knows?"

"Ask yourself, which side of the 'us' do you fall on? Because for years I tried to mask my identity, but for what reason?" She gave a small laugh. "Now, look at you. You've succeeded by embracing yours."

"But *I* didn't even know about this until now!" Casey objected.

"No, but you felt it deep inside your heart," she reassured

him. "And that's so much more important."

"This is a lot to absorb…and a lot to keep secret," Casey admitted. "Then again, no one would believe me even if I told them the truth." He paused for a long moment, thinking of how this information will permanently change his life, when a new question popped into his mind. "So you're really a water elemental, too?"

She nodded.

Casey scooted to the edge of the couch, his eager mind filled with questions. "Can you read the water like me? Is that how you knew what I painted in each of my pieces of art? I guess what I'm really wondering is, what abilities do you have?"

Her gray-blue eyes twinkled. "I thought you'd never ask."

CHAPTER NINE

Grandma Louise removed the afghan from her lap and set it on the armrest. She lifted herself off the couch and crossed the room, opening the top drawer of a cluttered desk. Beneath a bunch of old letters tucked in the back of the drawer, she pulled out a small, plain wooden box. She handed it to Casey.

"What's this?" he asked, flipping it over in his hand. It looked like a hand-carved jewelry box but possessed no distinguishing marks. He rubbed his finger over its smooth surface, coated in thick layers of shellac.

"Something that might help you to see the truth. Go on, open it," she prodded.

Casey lifted the lid and removed the soft layer of packaging on the inside, revealing a circular gold object. He placed the gold circle between his fingers and held it in front of his face. The circle glistened brightly like the sun as it caught the lamplight. "Is this what I think it is?" he asked, his eyes bulging with surprise.

Grandma Louise raised one silver eyebrow in a sign for him to continue his thoughts.

"It's pirate gold!" Casey exclaimed. He flipped this coin

over in his hand; it was probably the oldest object he had ever seen outside of a museum.

She smiled. "Actually, it's from a sunken Spanish galleon, but you're pretty close."

"Where did you buy it?" he wondered, his eyes fixated on the aged gold coin.

Grandma Louise gave a small chuckle. "You mean, where did I *find* it? I've never been a fan of fishing, so one time when we were on vacation in Florida, I decided to go for a little swim while your grandpa set his lines just offshore. I hadn't ventured far when something beneath our boat felt different like it called me down into the deeper waters. When I swam down to explore, I found this sunken ship intact."

Casey's jaw made its way to the floor. He shifted his gaze from the ancient artifact to his grandma and whispered with awe, "Didn't Grandpa worry about you?"

She shook her head and laughed with amusement. "Put a rod in that man's hand, and he would instantly get lost in time."

Casey turned the coin over in his hand, admiring the inherent beauty in its crude, misshapen edges. On one side, a simple, embossed crest—possibly the crest of Spain, he guessed—depicted a cross fashioned from two equal beams set perpendicular to each other, intersecting in the middle. In opposite corners of the cross, he noticed a crude drawing of a lion standing on its hind limbs, its front paws raised in the air and its tail curling high above its back. The other two corners contained an image that resembled a monarch's castle, with three rising towers and two windows above the open drawbridge, giving the uncanny resemblance to a frowning face with three sets of very spiky hair.

The other side of the coin almost looked like a tic-tac-toe board, but instead of using Xs and Os, random letters and numbers filled each space. When he read from left to right, it said something like, "L, 4, H," then on the next line, "P, V, A," with each of these letters ending in a period, and finally, "7, I, O." He found it hard to be certain since some parts of the coin seemed more worn than others. He also noticed a few raised dots around the crest and game board, surrounded by more letters that ran halfway off the edge of the coin.

"How deep did you go to find this?" he asked. Divers and treasure hunters had certainly discovered anything near the surface already. He doubted they would leave a single coin behind in their search for sunken loot.

She shrugged. "Pretty deep."

Casey raised a skeptical eyebrow. Talk about a vague response. "So, how long could you hold your breath?" he asked, testing another approach.

"A few minutes, I guess," she said in a nonchalant way. "I never timed it, of course."

"A few minutes!" Casey repeated, awestruck. In the summers, he'd seen his grandma swim a couple of laps in front of her dock. Nothing about her technique suggested she was a clandestine free diver. "You must be joking."

Her wrinkled lips drew into a flat line, showing no hint of humor whatsoever.

Casey couldn't decide which frightened him more: the impossible notion that his grandmother could dive to unimaginable depths on a single breath or the reality that she had actually accomplished that precise feat.

"So why don't you sell it?" he suggested, eager to change the subject. "I bet it's worth a fortune."

Grandma shrugged. "I thought I'd have to answer some uncomfortable questions about its origin. Questions I couldn't respond to without revealing details I never intended others to know. I never had the chance to pass this down to your father," she said and paused, releasing a weighted sigh, "so I'd like you to have it. You've been kind enough to share your art with me all these years, after all. This will be a reminder of *my* connection to the water. Besides, I think you need it now to help you believe all of this is real."

"Wow," Casey breathed. He flipped the coin over in his hand again, trying to visualize the feat his grandmother had just described in order to acquire this rare coin.

"Actually, I've never shown this find to anyone else but you. Not even your grandpa. So I guess it's our little secret now." She winked at Casey.

"Our little secret," Casey repeated with a slow nod. The implication of so many other secrets tied to this single coin. The pure existence of this object from a lost Spanish galleon opened the door to a whole new world. A world, his grandmother had reminded him, that threatened to destroy the fabric of the entire society.

"Did my father ever hear your story?" Casey wondered.

Grandma Louise shook her head, a deep sadness filling her eyes until they turned glassy in the light of the end table lamp. "I never made it that far. Like I told you before, he didn't take the news very well at all."

Casey thought about her response for a while. He knew so little about his father, almost like the subject was taboo to speak about at home. He learned long ago that asking questions about the man he didn't know only brought up sadness and despair. It was hard enough on his mom for her to endure him leaving her and their newborn son behind. Casey didn't need to make matters worse by dwelling on the past.

Yet now, his grandmother provided the perfect entrance into the unknown world of the man who walked out of his life before he even had a chance to know him. Here stood a chance to better understand the circumstances that had driven him away. And maybe, just maybe, the realization that Casey's arrival into their family wasn't the only reason he had left. Knowing that fact alone would ease much of the guilt he'd suffered all these years, believing he provided the sole reason Hugh Donnelly had abandoned them.

"What can you tell me about him?" Casey dared, hoping her tale wouldn't cause additional pain.

She blinked away the teary glaze, replacing it instead with a dreamy look that filled her eyes. She settled back into the couch, her fingers smoothing the blanket covering her legs as if remembering the days long past. "Your father used to water ski almost every day in the summer. He was very talented: he could complete tricks you'd never thought were possible on a set of skis. However, unlike some sports, there was little future for him. He tried out for a water skiing show and spent a year or so performing in southern Florida—that's when he met your mom, and they started dating—but he said he missed the change of season. That year spent in Florida felt like an eternal summer to him. Really, I think his heart dragged him back north. Your parents were so deeply in love that your mother resigned from her job to follow him here.

"Unfortunately, the change in location didn't help as much as he had hoped. He began to withdraw from others, eventually leading to reclusive and polarizing behaviors. He no longer received recognition for his talents like he had when he performed in front of cheering fans. And he quickly found he was ill-suited to a desk job working nine to five, so he retired early from corporate America. Shortly thereafter, he took a job as an office manager at a campground in Northern Minnesota. Now Hugh lives on meager wages and has adopted a minimalist lifestyle. I know it was a hard choice for him to make, but deep down, he didn't want to drag anyone else into his lot in life. He knew that was no way to raise a family."

* * * *

The rest of the day passed in a blur for Casey, spent mostly contemplating the tales she had shared as he bundled up and took Bo for a long walk across the thick lake ice, finding a recent snowmobile track to follow while the dog bounded through the deep drifts. As the sun sank early below the horizon, plunging the sky into swift darkness, he asked a barrage of questions while he helped Grandma Louise prepare dinner, then made a feeble attempt at homework, but it didn't really work. Instead, late that night, long after his grandmother had gone to bed, he picked the history book off the shelf and read through its pages again, imagining she repeated the stories that existed between the lines.

Satisfied the tales had permanently etched into his memory, he went back to his room and crawled into bed. Unfortunately, sleep did not come easily. For hours he lay awake on the mattress in the guest room, tossing from one side to the next as he mulled over the concept of the existence of elementals in the everyday world. He took the coin out of the plain box and flipped the gold treasure over in his hand. He shouldn't have believed a single word she told him. Her stories were too outlandish, too impossible for reality.

And yet, for some bizarre reason, they all seemed to make perfect sense.

He eventually set the gold coin in its box on his nightstand and lay back in bed, pulling the quilt and flannel sheets tight around him. Was it real? Or had she made up the whole story? Casey bet they sold replicas of pirate gold at every tourist trap in Florida and the Caribbean. It would have been so simple for her to concoct a fictitious tale to make him feel like he wasn't alone.

Outside, the brisk wintry wind whipped through bare branches. The howling wind sounded vastly different from the loud chirping of crickets that kept him awake on those hot summer nights. Tonight, however, the possibility of the truth behind this new revelation made sleep impossible.

Casey dug his phone out of his backpack, hoping he could verify her story with urban legends from the Internet. Like every other time he had visited Grandma Louise out here at the lake, he had no cellular reception. Frustrated, he wedged the phone deep into the side pocket of his backpack and zippered it closed.

The cell phone towers stood well out of range of her lakeside home, one of the reasons his grandmother kept an archaic modem connection through her telephone wire. She discouraged him from surfing the Internet during his visits since it tied up her landline, and she couldn't receive any incoming calls. "Go outside and enjoy the fresh air," she'd encourage him instead. In the summertime, Casey avoided the outdoors after dusk since he didn't wish to have the relentless mosquitoes — which had earned the comical nickname of "Minnesota's state bird" — devour every inch of his exposed flesh. Tonight, however, it was just too stinking cold. Plus, he didn't expect anyone to actually call at his grandma's house at this late hour, so she couldn't possibly object to him doing a little research to ease his mind. He tiptoed into the kitchen and pressed the start button on her computer.

"So glad we have Wi-Fi at home," Casey muttered, watching the dial-up Internet's spinning disc rotate about a hundred times. He drummed his fingers on the desk while waiting for a signal to connect. And once he did get a connection, every site took an excessively long time to load. He typed in the word "elemental," then set down the mouse and waited some more. In truth, he expected to find essentially nothing of interest, like when he had searched the word pairing of "water elly" before.

Instead, long lists of sites appeared. He clicked on the first option describing mythical and fantasy creatures.

Myth. Fantasy. Casey agreed completely with these terms. This whole thing was just a big joke, and he was losing his mind, wasn't he?

He scrolled through a few pictures of humanoid characters. One appeared glazed in a form-fitting sheet of ice. Another looked like its entire body sat immersed in flame. The colors resembled the ones he'd selected for his fire and ice paintings, but none of the descriptions seemed to match exactly. Ice elementals supposedly possessed the power to chill an attacker or generate deathly sharp spears of ice, while fire elementals allegedly set objects ablaze with a single touch. The site claimed ice elementals feared those with fire powers who could melt their icy weapons. Meanwhile fire elementals provided a weak defense against the water elementals, who could counteract a barrage of fireballs in a single splash, rendering their opponent ineffective. Earth elementals apparently summoned the forces inside certain rocks and used their brute strength to smash their opponents into fragments. Lastly, the air elementals assumed an amorphous shape like billowing cumulus clouds, which could stir up the winds to reach tornado speeds and whisk away their enemies, then drop them from an incredible height back to earth.

Casey shook his head, convinced another explanation must exist. Nothing matched the little he had already learned about elementals or "ellies," as Owen and Taylor called them. To him, the descriptions sounded more like characters in a video game or an epic fantasy Hollywood trilogy than the godlike historical figures from his grandma's book. Most importantly, everything he read on the Internet differed from what he had personally experienced...and was definitely nothing like the heat he saw emanating from Owen's lane in the pool. According to this site, water should counteract all of Owen's fire powers, rendering him completely ineffective. And it didn't sound anything like the mystery behind Taylor's fragile butterfly with wings of ice that had landed on Casey's nose. Her creation was beautiful yet simple, a testament to her mastery of the element. Not a destructive weapon aimed at another elemental to drain the living force from her intended target.

He tried to load another site, but the server kept spinning. Frustrated with his lack of helpful information from his research, Casey shut down the computer and returned to bed, pulling the warm covers tightly around his face to muffle the sound of the blustery winter gusts that carried across the frozen lake.

Still, sleep eluded him until the early hours of the morning, when he entered a dream world far different from any he had encountered before.

In his dream state, Casey's favorite painting of the crimson rip current along the Carolina coast had suddenly appeared inside his backpack. He took it out and hung it on his grandma's wall with a few of his early works. He adjusted the canvas, tilting it to the left so it would hang straight. But when he touched the center of the finished painting, his finger sank into the fresh cadmium red paint. Casey blinked, certain the canvas had been dry to the touch before he packed it on the trip. Otherwise, his entire backpack would be ruined from the acrylic paints.

Puzzled, he touched the canvas again. This time, his entire hand sank into the scarlet area on the canvas. He tried to remove his hand but couldn't escape the current's strong pull. He felt his feet leave the ground as the reddened water swirled around him, dragging him far away from the comfort of the bed in his grandma's guest room. Powerless against the swift current, he let the waters carry him, watching the familiar surroundings quickly drift into the distance. Casey turned around in the water, his attention focused on the direction he headed. Far away, he saw a small yellow object bobbing on the waves. "Jason's boogie board," Casey noted, recognizing its familiar shape from his painting.

He stretched out his arm toward the board, grateful for its buoyancy to keep his head above the surface, when the swirling, colorful eddies of ruby colored water dragged his feet under. Casey caught a quick gulp of air before his head submerged. Bubbles swirled around his head from the force of the undertow. He held the air in his ballooning cheeks, afraid to expel any of his precious, finite air supply.

As the water dragged him deeper below the surface, the color darkened from ruby to purple, then to a deep indigo blue. Few streams of sunlight filtered through the water column at this depth, casting a dim glow on his surroundings.

Casey wasn't sure how long he could hold his breath. Yet,

for some inexplicable reason, his finite supply of air didn't seem to pose a threat. Surrounded by the pressure of the deep, dark water, Casey felt strangely at ease.

Up ahead, he saw the dark outline of three tall masts of a massive sailing ship. It appeared hundreds of years old, like the majestic explorers' vessels from his grandma's history book.

The Spanish galleon. Inside, a thrill of adventure tugged at his heart. Had the ocean specifically chosen him to discover a secret held undisturbed for centuries?

A strange golden glow emanated from inside the sunken ship. The current deposited him on the ship's top deck, next to an old wooden chest. Its lid sat open wide, filled to the brink of overflowing with glowing treasure coins. Astonished with his find, Casey tried to lift the chest but found it impossible to budge. He gazed with wide hungry eyes at the untouched wealth of coins. He grabbed one of the gold coins, admiring the cross with lions embossed on one side and letters whose meaning he didn't comprehend on the other. Tempted to fill his pockets with the coins, Casey remembered the dwindling supply of air held within his cheeks. He settled for keeping just a single token of his discovery clutched tightly in one hand. With rapid kicks, he shot upward at an incredible speed, aiming for the surface. His exertion nearly exhausted the remaining air supply. Casey felt a wave of relief pass over him when the deep midnight blue waters brightened into lighter shades, touched by the sun's midday rays. He was almost there.

Yet, for some bizarre reason, Casey couldn't reach the surface. He kicked and pulled, inching closer to the needed source of air but unable to achieve his target. Once immersed in its realm, Casey found it impossible to escape his element, like the ocean refused to reveal its secrets hidden in the deep.

Suddenly, the water around him grew inexplicably hot. Casey thrashed with confusion, spinning his head wildly from one side to the other when he caught the sound of familiar laughter ringing through the water. He turned and glimpsed Owen Teague swimming past, a citrus glow of water in his wake. Still grasping the coin, Casey ignored his desperate desire for a breath of fresh air and sprinted forward to catch him. His hand touched the side a finger length behind Owen.

Casey's chest heaved when he finally broke the surface of the water, letting his hand rest on the side of the pool.

"Nice try, water elly," Owen cackled.

Panting, Casey flew up in bed and kicked off the flannel sheet and covers. His heart pounded against his ribcage, faster and louder than the grandfather clock's steady beat. Beads of sweat soaked his brow and stained the front of his shirt and along his spine. His eyes darted madly from side to side as he struggled to orient himself. He began to register the familiar surroundings of the bed and futon, lace curtains and nightstand piled high with his books, reminders of his grandmother's guest room.

"It was just a dream," he reassured himself, his breaths gradually returning to a normal pace. His skin, wet with perspiration, felt cool and clammy as his racing pulse began to subside. He opened his palm, shocked to find the ancient gold coin clutched tightly in his palm. Had he happened to fall asleep with it inside his grasp and imagined his descent toward the ship's wreckage? Or had he managed to remove it from the box in his dreamlike trance? He shook his head, uncertain of the truth, and gently placed the coin back inside its wooden box on the nightstand, making a mental note to return it to his grandma in the morning. He wasn't ready to accept all of this yet, and the coin represented solid evidence of a world he still didn't fully believe existed.

A part of him wished he'd brought his paints and canvas to capture the sensations of his dream while they were fresh in his mind, but he had intentionally left them at home, thinking he would spend all of his free time preparing for upcoming exams. He opened one of his notebooks and ripped out a piece of lined paper, and dug a pencil from the bottom of his backpack to sketch the memory instead. His pencil breezed over the paper as he drew rough lines for the crimson current that dragged him to the ocean's depths, dimly lit in the filtered sunlight from above. A trio of simple crosses at the bottom represented the three masts on the sunken Spanish galleon, and a radiating glow from the golden coins of precious cargo that remained onboard. Casey made a few notes in the margins to help him recall the sensations he felt of temperature, color, and scents: sensations only he could understand.

With his mind calmed and his body exhausted, Casey dropped into a solid, dreamless sleep.

CHAPTER TEN

Bo woke Casey the next morning with an excited lick across the face.

"Unghh." Casey's voice came out garbled, drugged with sleep. He wiped off the dog slobber with the back of his hand and rolled to his other side, hoping to prevent another wakeup call.

Bo sprang onto the bed and spun around twice, searching for a comfortable spot to plop down alongside Casey's legs. His tail thumped repeatedly, hitting the guest room wall like a metronome keeping time.

Grandma Louise popped her head in through the door. "Good morning, sunshine," she warbled, then walked across to the windows to draw back the lacy curtains. Bright winter rays poured into the room, giving the false perception of heat and warmth from the distant sun.

Casey pulled the covers up over his head for his reply.

He heard his grandmother say, "I'm sorry to have to wake you, especially when I'm pretty sure all of this kept you up too late last night, but it's almost eleven in the morning, and your mom just called to say she's already on her way to come and pick you up. She'll be here in about forty-five minutes, so I thought you might want some food before you go."

Whack. Whack. Whack. Bo's happy, thumping tail provided the only sound in the room.

"I can make you breakfast…or lunch…or even brunch, for that matter. Whatever you'd like," she offered kindly.

At the sound of those words, Bo's tail fell suddenly still.

Casey peeked out from under the covers, wondering if the dog really could understand his grandmother's intent.

Bo's mouth dropped open, panting with anticipation. Apparently, he could.

"The food's for him, Bo. You already ate your breakfast," she clarified.

Bo clamped his jaw shut and laid his head on his paws, giving the impression of a sulking child.

Grandma Louise rolled her eyes. "Anyway, what would you like me to make you, Casey?"

He shrugged, unwilling to trust his voice to words. Maybe he could forget about food altogether and stay in bed for the next forty-five minutes, pretending none of yesterday's events had happened. Then he could go back home and resume his normal life.

Grandma Louise sighed. He heard her body sink into the futon couch across the room. "I know it was a lot to take in. I get that. And I'm sorry to dump all of this on you at once. But in the long run, I'm positive you'll view this as a talent. A gift. Something that separates you from others and makes you special."

Slowly, Casey sat up to face her. He gazed into his grandmother's twilight blue eyes, wondering if the words she spoke truly came from her heart. He hadn't thought of it that way before. Up until that point, the diagnosis of synesthesia had made him feel different from his family and an oddity compared to his peers. Sure, it gave him an advantage in the water, but it also clouded his mind with bizarre combinations of senses.

He'd found the only way he could purge these feelings from his thoughts was to allow the colors to manifest themselves on the canvas. It didn't account for the scents or tastes, but it was a start.

Suddenly a new possibility surfaced, one that Casey had deliberately driven away countless times in the past.

"I think I should see him," Casey blurted, finally voicing the single thought that had tugged at the back of his mind for the majority of his life. "It might help this all make so much more sense. He's my father. He owes that much to me."

Grandma Louise looked at him for a long moment, her expression suddenly filling with a mixture of compassion and overwhelming sadness…and perhaps a trace of pity, too. Finally, she spoke, her voice a soft whisper. "I can see why you'd want to. But when you go and see your father, be sure to take Bo with you. He might ease Hugh's temper by reminding him of his childhood water dog."

* * * *

"How was your weekend?" Ellen asked before Casey even had a chance to close the door to the car against the bitter cold outside. She gave a friendly wave to Grandma Louise, then completed her three-point turn to head out the driveway.

"Fine," Casey groaned. He suspected his mom would launch into the twenty questions game as soon as she had the chance. He reached into the glove box and grabbed a spare pair of sunglasses to shield his eyes from the blinding snow glare that felt harsher than normal in his exhausted state.

She peeked over at him. "Did you enjoy seeing Grandma?"

Casey forced a convincing nod. "Yep."

"Was it relaxing to spend some time up at the lake?" she asked.

"Yeah," he lied, wondering if his time with Grandma Louise had only made matters worse.

"Did you finish your homework?"

"Sure."

"Want to stop for food on the way home?"

"Nah."

Casey cringed at the selfishness of his lethargic, monosyllabic responses. In hindsight, he wished he had asked his grandmother a few more of the thousands of questions that bombarded his mind after he woke up late in the morning. At the time, he found it difficult to voice his emotions in his sleep-deprived state. Now he thirsted for answers, especially to his unsettling dream, and he couldn't utter a single word.

He had predicted the ride home with his mom would seem awkward, knowing the truth about himself and Hugh and not being able to share any of it with her—if Grandma Louise's story held true, of course. Still, he knew he must keep this a secret from his mom.

To be honest, he wasn't sure what to do with this news about having elemental abilities. He also couldn't predict how she'd react when he asked to visit his father, especially when he doubted she had heard from him in years.

Casey gazed out the window, imagining he clutched the coin in his hand like he had in the vivid dream. Despite Grandma Louise's insistence, he had refused to take the coin home with him. He didn't want to relive the nightmare of his entrapment in the deep waters, unable to break through to the surface. Plus, he had no idea what he would say if his mom ever found the treasure coin in his room. He decided it wasn't worth the risk. Instead, he had tucked his pencil sketch into the back pocket of his jeans. It must serve as the sole reminder of his grandmother's disclosure of inherited elemental powers for now. He made a mental note to give that painting to her once completed.

As they drove further away from Grandma Louise's lake home and within range of more cell towers, Casey's phone emitted several irritated buzzes. He glanced at his screen, surprised to find a series of unanswered texts from Taylor Sperry.

"Sounds like somebody missed you," his mom chuckled.

"Ha," Casey said, glad his mom didn't elaborate on the topic. Still, the knowledge that she suspected a girl had texted him multiple times while he was gone made his cheeks grow warm.

"Gimme a sec," he told her and clicked on Taylor's name.

"Well, that's sure an improvement. At least I got more than a one-word response this time," his mom noted with a hint of sarcasm.

Casey rolled his eyes, then read through the stream. Each line appeared in its own distinct green box with rounded corners. The first messages came early on Saturday morning.

How are you? Doing ok with the news?

I have a game today at 3. R U coming to watch me again?

Around dinnertime, she had sent another text.

Looked for you after the game. Were U there? Guess i missed u.

Late last evening, she'd written....

Surprised I haven't heard from you yet. Did i scare u?

Then early this morning, the last of her messages read....

U know, if someone gives you her number, it's considered polite to ACTUALLY use it!

She sounded pretty disgusted with him. He quickly typed up an apology, certain she would think it was a pretty lame excuse, and he should get a better cell phone provider.

Sorry. Up north all weekend. Out in the boonies = no service :(

His phone buzzed a few seconds later with her reply.

That's cool. Thought maybe u were trying to avoid me.

He chuckled under his breath and let his thumbs fly over the screen, grateful she was still talking to him after all of his mistakes in elementary school and now this new mishap.

As if. Had to go to grandmas. Found out you were right. Guess I'm not the only e after all. He made sure to use her designated abbreviation for "elly" before pressing the send button.

Taylor got back to him right away.

E often runs in the family.

Casey quickly typed his response. *Don't know what 2 think anymore. It changes everything. Don't know what im supposed to do.*

His response startled him, seeing the sincerity in his words actually in print. How did it affect him as an athlete? Worse, how did this news change his perception of the world and his role in it?

Calm down. Meet me at spring hill playground in 15 min.

The Spring Hill Elementary School playground? Her response surprised Casey. He was pretty sure there were a few incidents on that very same playground that had infuriated her over the years. Incidents he hadn't realize involved elemental abilities until now.

Can't. I'm driving home from up north.

Okay, then call me ASAP. C U soon.

Sure thing.

At least one good thing came out of this. Taylor wasn't mad at him anymore. He sighed, grateful for one friend in whom he could confide.

"Everything okay?" his mom asked. The tone of her voice offered him yet another opportunity to voice the myriad thoughts cluttering his mind.

"Yeah," Casey replied, deciding to take her up on the offer…in a non-assuming way, of course. "Hey, Mom, have you ever heard of elementals?" He kept his gaze focused on the straight stretch of black asphalt in front of them, grateful for the sunglasses to hide his eyes. He tried to keep his uncertain emotions from seeping into his voice to make his mom grow suspicious.

"Elementals?" she asked. "No, but I've heard of the four elements. Aristotle or one of those other famous Greek philosophers described all matter as being composed of one of the four elements: earth, air, water, and fire. Why do you ask?"

"Oh, it's just from a book I'm reading," Casey replied quickly. "I was only wondering if you had heard of people having elemental powers. That's all."

"You mean in real life?" his mom clarified.

"Sure, I guess," Casey said, trying to keep a flat tone.

"Hmm. Let me think for a minute," she said.

On long car rides, Casey would often asked random questions to get his mom started on some bizarre tangents. It definitely made the time pass more quickly, and he usually learned something new. Right now, he imagined her mind scanning through the thousands of news stories she had filed away in her memory over the years, all in an attempt to keep her student engaged in current events. He sometimes wondered if her career teaching American and world history was practically synonymous with "news junkie."

"Oh, okay. I've got something that might work," she said, her voice filled with sudden enthusiasm. A smile lit her face as he imagined the gears shifted inside her head, distracting her from his recent sullen behavior. Casey suspected she might enjoy these mental detours as much as he did to reduce the monotony of the drive. "We'll start with the earth, okay?"

Casey figured her question was rhetorical. Once she got going, she barely paused for a breath.

"I've read that some animals are reported to leave their homes before an earthquake like they can sense the tremors inside the earth days before a quake ravages an area. Bees will leave their hives, chickens will stop laying eggs, and even rats and snakes will leave their homes."

"That's pretty cool," Casey admitted. "But what about humans?"

"Some humans are said to be 'earth sensitive' and will feel dizzy or nauseous before an earthquake strikes an area," she added.

"So they can feel the shifting tectonic plates?"

"Possibly. Or maybe they're able to pick up magnetic anomalies inside the earth. It's hard to say." She spoke quickly, keeping her eyes trained on the black stretch of road, shimmering in the midday brightness.

Casey couldn't mask the skepticism in his voice. "Okay, but what about one of the other four elements?"

"How about this? For air, some yogis practice meditation that allows them to supposedly levitate off the ground," his mom continued.

"For real?" Casey's eyes opened wide.

"Yep. If you watch videos of them, their robes will be flapping in the breeze beneath them as they sit cross-legged in the air, using only a stick held in one hand."

"So, they're putting all of their weight on the stick?"

"No. Not at all," she explained. "It's more like it's used for a reference point. People will wave their hands underneath them and everything, trying to figure out how they can sit several feet off the ground like they are fixed in a trance."

"How do you think they can levitate?" Casey wondered. "They have air powers?"

His mom shrugged. "I'm not exactly sure. Some people say it's transcendental meditation. Others say it's simple physics like in a circus act."

"Okay, I admit that's pretty cool. So what do you know about water?" he asked, his voice rising a note in eager anticipation.

"I actually can think of a couple of very different examples for this element."

Casey sat up straighter in his seat, hoping she hadn't noticed his sudden change in interest.

Ellen began, "Well, the obvious one you probably already guessed are the record-breaking free divers who can travel to unimaginable depths on a single breath."

Casey stopped breathing for a moment. The image from his nightmare of the sunken Spanish galleon flashed through his mind. But instead of him diving down to the shipwreck, he envisioned Grandma Louise prying open the wooden chest and pulling out a single golden coin. "They must be able to hold their breath a long time," he wagered, thinking an affirmative would make his grandma's story that much more plausible.

"A remarkably long time," she agreed. "Some can stay underwater for three or four minutes, but I think I read that the record is over twenty-two minutes."

Casey gasped. "You're joking."

"I know," his mom nodded. "It sounds completely unbelievable, doesn't it? I mean, it's not always safe. Sometimes, the divers blackout underwater, so they might not even make it back to the surface at all. Still, they're able to train their bodies to dive to remarkable depths: several hundred feet or more."

"Wow." Casey thought about holding his breath for that duration of time while the water pressure at greater depths squeezed his lungs in its tight embrace. The mere thought seemed impossible to fathom. How long could Grandma Louise stay underwater when she was younger? He bet her time might have even rivaled some of the champion free divers if she truly had water elemental powers like she had claimed.

"There's another case I can think of that's completely unrelated," she continued, "but also might fit what you're looking for. Sometimes in drought-stricken areas like southern California, farmers will ask water witches to help them drill for a new well."

"They're really witches?" Casey asked.

"They're actually called dowsers, though most people call them water witches because they 'witch' the land."

Casey scrunched his nose with confusion. "How do they do that?"

"For hundreds of years, dowsers claimed they could sense the underground water using their intuition and a rod or stick," she elaborated.

"Oh, I think I've seen a picture of that before. Is it like

when they walk through a field with a Y-shaped twig and wait for it to bob up and down?" Casey guessed.

"Exactly. Some of the water witches say they have a natural gift. They claim you're either born with the gift or you're not."

Casey nodded. So many similarities rang through his head with this example. A natural gift, just like Grandma Louise had described in her stories from the old history book.

Ellen added, "I guess they can tell all sorts of information about the water, like how deep it is, whether it's contaminated or not, how much water it could produce, you get the idea."

"So how do they know? Do their rods just starts to bounce up and down or something?"

"Yes. And sometimes they claim they can feel it in their skin." She peeked at him to gauge his reaction.

"Weird," Casey noted, wondering if their ability to feel the water in their skin differed much from his ability to read the water and find the best pathway to follow in his races. He began to think these new examples better supported his grandmother's stories. Maybe there was some truth to her tales after all.

"Scientists will counter that there's groundwater everywhere," his mom continued, "if you dig deep enough. But many of the farmers believe they find true success using the water witches' advice instead. In fact, some may call them modern day superheroes."

"So you think these people are all examples of elementals?" he dared. He pulled his sunglasses down the bridge of his nose, studying the sincerity in her face as she responded.

"Honestly, I don't believe we are able to explain every facet of our world," she admitted. "Science is always changing over time — that's essentially the definition of evolution. But there are still some things that remain unexplained. I think we'll figure it out eventually. We're just not there yet."

Casey pondered her examples. The stories were remarkable indeed. Whether these people actually possessed elemental powers, he couldn't say for sure, but it was some sort of gift or talent that enabled them to achieve these seemingly impossible feats.

She added, "Maybe it's skill, maybe sheer luck. I wouldn't go so far as to say they have powers within those elements, but I will admit it's definitely something I don't fully grasp. You might also think of it like a bell curve." She removed one hand from the steering wheel to trace the graph's familiar shape in the air. Her line in space closely resembled the outline of the Liberty Bell with a rounded top. "Statistics tell us that the majority of the population resides within one standard deviation away from the norm. Once you go two standard deviations away, you're looking at ninety-five percent of the population fitting in the definition of 'normal.' And three standard deviations away, and you're already over ninety-nine percent of the population lying under the bell curve."

"So, what exactly does that mean?" Casey asked.

"I like to think of it like this: on every spectrum on human abilities, most of the people in the world would fall into the normal range. Still, some have abilities that make them special and are able to withstand extremes, like holding your breath for twenty-two minutes."

Casey appreciated that explanation: some people have abilities that make them special. Maybe his grandma was right, and it wasn't synesthesia like the doctors had suggested, but rather a special ability triggered by the water. Did that necessarily make him a water elly? He didn't exactly know the answer to that question, although he'd love to find out for certain.

"We still have one more element to go," his mom said with enthusiasm. Casey imagined she often used her incessant passion for current events to keep her energetic middle school students engaged all day. "Fire...." She paused briefly for effect. "I'm not sure you're going to believe me, but there are stories worldwide of spontaneous human combustion."

Casey gaped at her with surprise. He'd never actually heard those words used together in reference to a human. "What do you mean?" he asked, certain he had misheard her.

"The victim, in this case, a human, suddenly and spontaneously ignites, even though their surroundings remain untouched."

"Get out," Casey whispered in disbelief.

"No, really. Some of them have even lived after the event, but most of the time, they can only find the charred remains as the body burns from the inside out," she said.

"How does that happen? I mean, how does somebody suddenly catch on fire?" he wondered. "Isn't the human body mostly made up of water? It doesn't seem like it would be easy to ignite water."

"You're right. Maybe in some of the cases, the victim dropped a cigarette or candle onto their clothes without realizing it. Others speculate there might be some agent inside the body that could cause it to burn in the presence of an ignition source, like a spark of fire. Fat provides an excellent fuel source, and hair is extremely flammable. Or maybe acetone, like nail polish remover, might build up in excess when someone is ill, and that chemical can catch flame readily."

Casey blinked, looking at her incredulously. "And how exactly do you remember all of this information?" he wondered.

She shrugged, her lips turning up in a delighted grin. "These stories pop up in the news from time to time. Some of them just happen to stick in my head better than others, I suppose."

Casey thought back to his string of texts from Taylor. "What about ice elementals?"

"I don't know," she admitted. "I mean, ice isn't one of the four elements."

Casey envisioned the butterfly landing on his nose, its delicate wings intricately fashioned from beautiful ice crystals.

She gave a small gasp as a novel idea sprang into her head.

"But wasn't Disney's movie, *Frozen*, based off a Hans Christian Andersen fairy tale called *The Snow Queen*?"

Casey shrugged. "I don't know. Maybe."

"I'm pretty sure it was. Meaning, it's possible the tale was rooted in some semblance of the truth."

His mom was quiet for a while. Casey stared out the window, wondering how in the world of snow and ice around him, the abilities could be limited to only the original four elements. How could Taylor accomplish those remarkable feats if she didn't have a connection to ice itself?

"Y'know," his mom said, breaking the silence, "I think I have heard of some remarkable stories of people who seem to be invulnerable to the snow and ice. I remember reading about a man who claimed he could control his body's responses to the cold. It was pretty amazing. When most people would experience hypothermia or frostbite, he was perfectly fine. Like on Mount Everest: many climbers have died from exposure to the elements, but he climbed the mountain in nothing but shorts and sandals. He said he used an ancient form of meditation from the Himalayas that was supposed to produce enough heat inside your body to melt the ice around you, even when the temperature outside was well below freezing. Or those swimmers that can cross the English Channel without a wetsuit. I think I remember reading that one of them even went on to swim between icebergs in Antarctica. The human body is an amazing thing, and the mind, even more so."

"That is pretty amazing," Casey said with a low whistle.

"I agree. Can you imagine willing yourself to feel warmer, even when it's freezing outside like today?"

He shook his head. "No. The sun always seems deceptively warm on these bright days, but in reality, the temperature is brutally cold."

Casey noticed they had reached the city limits for the neighboring town of Great Plains. Thanks to his mom's stories, the trip had passed at an incredible speed. At this rate, they'd be home in no time.

"What book were you reading, anyway?" his mom wondered.

"Huh? Oh…." His mind pictured the hardbound cover and the musty smell that filled his nostrils every time he flipped a yellowed page. He remembered the website on the old computer that read *myth, fantasy*. He needed to come up with something believable…and fast. "Um, just some old fantasy book at Grandma's house, that's all."

"Well, I'm glad to hear you're reading for pleasure, but I hope you spent some time on your homework. So what three tests do you have this week?" she asked.

Casey gulped. He'd forgotten all about his exams. "Math, science, and health. Bio's tomorrow," he said with a delayed response.

"Need any help?" she offered kindly.

Casey shook his head. His mom had stopped being able to help him with his math years ago. She was still willing to try, but Casey usually ended up having to re-teach her everything. He felt it had become a pointless exercise in testing his patience, and he had better ways to allocate his time in preparation. "No, thanks. I'm good," he replied with false confidence.

Inside, his mind clouded with worry. How was he supposed to focus on his upcoming tests and swim meets when the newfound existence of elementals weighed heavily on his mind? Worse, how could he carry on with his normal daily life knowing that his grandma claimed he held elemental powers? It seemed too much to grasp all at once. As Casey contemplated his possibilities, one course of action rose above the others in logic and reasoning, but he didn't dare consider choosing that extreme pathway.

Not yet, at least.

CHAPTER ELEVEN

When they got home, Casey headed straight up the stairs to his room to unpack. His painting of the crimson rip current and the stack of canvases in the corner of his room automatically drew his gaze. He set down his bags and flipped through the paintings, one by one. How couldn't he have realized sooner? Why did he believe that synesthesia alone could possibly explain all of his abilities with water?

He set the paintings back in their stack, leaving the rip current canvas on top, then threw his dirty clothes in a pile for laundry and opened his school backpack. A part of him wished he'd actually attempted to study while gone at Grandma's. Still, he promised Taylor he'd get in touch with her as soon as he got home. Ignoring his unfinished work, he slipped his phone from his pocket and called her number.

"Hey, Taylor. It's Casey."

"What's up?" she asked brightly.

Judging by her tone, she sounded much happier to talk to him now than she had after her hockey game. Casey breathed a sigh of relief. "Sorry to get back to you so late," he apologized. "I just got home."

"So, how'd it go?" Taylor asked in a leading voice.

"My trip to Grandma's?" he wondered.

"And the 'e' stories," she added.

"Oh. That." He sighed again. His mind still reeled from the jolt to his perception of normality. His glance fell on his painting again, spotting the yellow speck representing Jason's boogie board, far out at sea. That day on the beach, people told him he shouldn't have been able to escape, much less save his cousin from its strong pull. All this time, Casey had thought that particular event had inspired him to begin his swimming career. Who would have thought he possessed an inherent connection to the water? How should he have known that water elementals even existed?

He realized he never responded to Taylor's prompt about the stories he heard of elementals. "Let's just say they were really unexpected."

"Are you doing okay?" she asked sympathetically.

He shrugged. "Yeah, I guess."

"You sound like you need to get it off your chest. Go on. Spill," she encouraged him.

He tilted his head sideways. Hadn't she cautioned him about talk of ellies? "Now?" he asked, surprised. "Aren't you afraid someone's bugging your phone?"

"Ha!" Taylor laughed. "You're funny. Seriously, though. I'm here for you."

Casey blinked. Just the other day, she was livid with him for coming to her game. She'd given him a strict warning before abandoning him down by the pond. "Really? Are you sure?"

"Absolutely," she said to him with confidence.

"But, Taylor, I don't get it. The other night after your game, you sounded so mad at me...and now you actually want to talk?"

"You don't know how hard it is to always keep this a

secret. And maybe that's part of the reason you infuriated me so much throughout elementary school. You were the person I should have had the best chance of relating to. But you were completely clueless. I guess I was a little jealous that you didn't carry this burden like I did. You didn't have to worry all the time that someone would notice just how different you were because you had absolutely no idea yourself." She sighed. "It's just such a relief to get this off my chest and have someone to finally share it with. Even if that someone is you."

"Gee. Thanks," Casey said in a flat voice, not sure if he should take that as a compliment.

She amended her statement, "I mean 'cause you're my polar opposite and all. Not because it's *you*."

"I don't know if that's making me feel any better," Casey admitted.

"Oh, stop. You know what I mean."

Casey remained cautious. "Aren't you worried I'll tell someone?"

"Nope. Not at all," she replied.

Still, something didn't make sense to Casey. "I thought you said before that you switched schools because of me. I'm pretty sure you called me a 'liability.'"

Taylor laughed. "Yeah, but that was before you knew about yourself. Now everything's different."

Casey said, "How so?"

"Because you're also a competitive athlete, and now you actually know. You're in the same boat as me...sorry, no water pun intended. But it's true. If you talk, you'll run the risk of jeopardizing your whole future in swimming. People think you've gotten this far on sheer talent and hard work. And once they find out—if they even believe your story in the first place—you might lose out on recruitment and scholarship opportunities," she announced in a matter-of-fact tone.

Suddenly, Casey began to second-guess his worthiness

for his accomplishments. Maybe Taylor was right, and he didn't actually deserve any of the records he'd broken. He had been given the gift of reading the water, so he wasn't on the same stage as everyone else. Almost like he'd cheated himself to victory all of those years.

"I hadn't thought of it that way before," Casey admitted. His heart filled with guilt when he realized more than his unworthy achievements burdened his mind. He also felt extremely uncomfortable for deceiving his mom. She had listed numerous examples of people with extraordinary abilities, and he'd spun the whole reason for his interest on a work of fiction. He knew he had no choice; he couldn't risk exposing a world he knew so little about to anyone outside the elemental community. He had to bear one secret he couldn't share with his mother, no matter how much it pained him to hide something this big.

"Sorry to burst your bubble. Oh! Guess I let another water elly pun slip there." Taylor laughed playfully.

Casey grimaced. It felt like a block of ice had walloped him straight in the heart, diminishing his years of hard work and effort in a single blow. He probably deserved it, though, for everything he'd put her through over the years. Still, he had to admit it hurt.

"Have you ever wondered if it's something else?" he asked.

"What do you mean? Like, not elly powers?"

Casey explained. "Exactly. My doctor first diagnosed me with synesthesia, or a fusion of senses he claimed allowed me to read a book in a variety of colors or smell chocolate chip cookies fresh out of the over whenever I went to the pool, or —"

Taylor interrupted him with a snicker. "You smell home-baked cookies at the pool?"

"Yeah," he admitted, suddenly self-conscious about his admission.

"Most people can't get past the overwhelming odor of

chlorine even walking past the pool doors, and you walk inside and smell *cookies*?" Her voice peaked on the last word like she could barely contain her hilarity.

"I guess," he said, disheartened by her reaction.

"That's cute. Seriously," she said before erupting into full-blown laughter.

"I always thought it was because it reminded me of home," Casey explained innocently.

Taylor laughed. "So what happens when you go to the lake? Do you smell cookies there, too?" she teased.

"No. I get a taste in my mouth like I've just eaten ripe, juicy peaches and had a glass of strawberry lemonade."

"Okay, that's pretty cool," Taylor said. He could hear her licking her lips for effect. "And what about the ocean?"

"It's caramel popcorn with a hint of sea salt."

"Okay, but kinda boring, don't you think?" she commented. "Too predictable."

"Sorry," Casey said in a tone that didn't sound the least bit apologetic. So now she was judging him based on his fusion of senses that lay completely outside his control?

"What else have you got for me?" she asked.

Casey paused for a moment, trying to think of how to explain his other senses associated with water. "Well, the word 'pool' shimmers in a sapphire blue color whenever I see it in print."

"Sweet. And…?" she prompted.

"The word 'lake' looks a light purple, and the word 'sea' a deep pink."

"Every time you see it written out?"

"Yep. Every time."

"Even if I write it by hand?"

"Anyway," Casey said, intentionally avoiding her question. "Before you got me off topic, I had a question for you."

"Shoot."

He shifted his phone to his other ear before continuing. "Have you ever wondered if instead of having elly powers, it's just an extreme version of normal?"

"What do you mean?"

"Like on a bell curve," Casey said. "Have you seen one before?"

"Yes, I remember studying them in math," she noted.

"If the area in the middle is considered normal," he said, finding himself drawing the familiar shape in the air to help him explain, even though she couldn't see his graph, "you can imagine that most of the population falls within the normal range. But on the edges, you would get the extremes. Do you think the elly powers lie in the extremes?" he asked. "Or maybe they're not elemental powers at all, but simply variations of the normal spectrum of abilities."

Taylor thought for a while. "Or maybe the ellies always fall on the outside because of their powers. That way, they could still look like extreme versions of what's considered normal."

Casey scratched his head. It reminded him of the chicken and the egg quandary. Each side had a viable reason as to why they came first.

He had trouble focusing on the remainder of their conversation, his mind muddled with puzzling and contradictory facts to everything he'd learned his entire life. Even after hanging up the phone, he wondered how this entire clandestine world had existed for thousands of years, even up until present day. More confusing yet, how could he be a part of this world without previously knowing it himself?

* * * *

That night Casey lay awake in bed, thinking. Owen, he barely knew, but Grandma Louise and Taylor had never given him any reason to doubt them in the past.

He thought back to his initial fear and distrust when he explained how he could see the current and read the water.

Scientists had hypothesized that his neurons from one sensory system bridged the synapses to another, allowing him to cross his connections and make associations between different senses. Parts of his brain that usually remained distinct had become intertwined. His doctor told him that many of these neural pathways crossed in childhood but typically disappeared later in life. His pathways simply happened to remain crossed in a highly consistent manner, creating a fusion of vastly distinct senses.

That scientific reason explained so many things, like why entering the pool always smelled like warm chocolate chip cookies, while a dip in the lake tasted like peaches and strawberry lemonade. The condition of synesthesia also accounted for why his biology reading appeared in a rainbow of neon colors and why the word "pool" always looked sapphire blue, as if shimmering in the bright midday sun.

The doctor further explained that sometimes sounds associated with certain colors or textures associated with certain noises. Maybe saving his cousin, Jason, had unlocked Casey's innate ability to read the water. Unlike the monochromatic blue he had expected, the water appeared in a rainbow of colors to depict different currents and swirling eddies. Casey soon learned to recognize the path of least resistance stretching before him, denoted in a beautiful blue-green. He realized his perception of the water was far unlike that of others around him, giving him an advantage in the pool. Only his paintings provided a window into his mind, allowing others to see what he saw underwater...if they were willing to see his work for something beyond abstract art.

All this time, Casey had believed the diagnosis. The biological explanation for his condition made sense. Now, to learn his abilities heralded from an entirely different source not only stunned him originally, it made him question the whole supposed world of elementals altogether.

From the moment his mother had given him a quizzical

look when he described the crimson color of the rip current that dragged Jason out to sea, Casey had realized he didn't see the water the same way as everyone else. He began to wonder if everyone even possessed the same interpretation of colors. Did his version of blue-green look the same as her idea of that color? Or did something others perceived as blue really look like more like his impression of the color orange? Could that explain why he viewed the water in a different way? These questions, paired with his diagnosis of synesthesia, had spawned his initial interest in neuroscience as a possible career path.

Now he doubted everything, including the validity of his future career. He had thought a different perception of colors might explain why the rip current looked red to him and no one else. He assumed it was simply a different interpretation of the same event.

If you gave him a hundred guesses, Casey never would have considered the powers of a water elly could create these possibilities. The idea was preposterous like something imagined in a fantastical fairy tale.

And yet....

Casey might not have trusted Owen, but when Grandma Louise and Taylor told him the same thing, it became more challenging for him to dispute or ignore the theory. How could the elementals have impacted history in a way that scholars and historians had not formally documented? How could Grandma Louise claim to have the ability to dive to incredible depths to retrieve an ancient gold coin from a sunken ship? Or how could Taylor create impossible works from ice, then control them to her whim if she didn't possess a secret gift?

He mulled over these baffling ideas and questions in his mind. Many hours passed before sleep eventually found him.

* * * *

He woke the next morning to his bedroom door flying open. "Ohmigosh! Casey, I can't believe you're still in bed. You'll

be late for school!" his mom declared in a shrill voice and flipped
on the bright overhead light.

Casey groaned and rolled over in bed, pulling his covers
up over his head to shield his face from the light's shocking
intensity.

"Not today," she said and crossed the room in three quick
strides to reach his bed. "It's ten below, and I don't want you
waiting at the bus stop. I'll drop you off on my way to work, but
I need you to get going. I have a meeting this morning."

"Fine," Casey consented and threw the covers back. The
idea of waiting outside in the bitter cold for a bus that notoriously
showed up late did not sound the least bit appealing.

His mom crossed her arms over her chest and studied
his weary face. "You know, this weekend was supposed to be
relaxing. A chance for you to take a break from everything. How
are you feeling today?"

"I dunno," he said, his words garbled with drowsiness.

"By the way, didn't you say you have a biology test
today?" she reminded him.

"Thanks for reminding me," Casey said, heavy on the
sarcasm. He crawled out of bed and grabbed his bag, still in the
same condition as when he'd gotten home yesterday. His attempts
at studying proved fruitless, so he had avoided it altogether. Now
he greatly regretted that decision.

"And good luck in your last home meet. I'll be cheering
for you," she added when she pulled up in front of Westlake
High School's main entrance, her voice bright and sunny despite
the frigid temperatures outside.

Casey pulled his hood up over his head before daring to
open the passenger door. He gave a weighted groan and mumbled
a thanks before trudging toward the front entrance. The early
morning darkness and biting wind made him wish he'd chosen
to spend the rest of the day in bed. With every breath, the icy
air pierced his throat, the crystals stinging his lungs as if he had

inhaled shards of glass. What a way to start his day.

Drained from his restless sleep, Casey scolded himself for how the weekend had turned out. He should have been well prepared for his exams and last home meet, but his body felt exhausted and his energy stores depleted. He wasn't sure how he'd manage to last all day.

Unfortunately, biology class proved even worse. As soon as he slogged through the door, Mandi greeted him with an amiable wave. "Good luck in your last home meet today!" she said cheerily.

Casey felt bad when his grogginess made his voice sound more like a caveman's grunt than a coherent reply.

Mandi's face scrunched up, her eyes crinkling with repulsion. She gave him a withered half-smile, then quickly turned to Christina Loveland and whispered something too low for Casey to hear.

Casey grimaced. He had single-handedly destroyed any remaining trace of interest she had in him. However, he didn't have much time to ponder her reaction when Mrs. Davidson passed out the exams three seconds after the bell rang to start class. Despite his lack of studying, Casey was fairly sure he knew everything, although he had the greatest difficulty with the section on aquatic ecology since the words kept jumping off the page in a variety of colors that made it extremely difficult to concentrate. He managed to finish the last short response questions a moment before the bell rang.

He leapt up to turn in his exam and catch Mandi to apologize. She didn't even glance his way before marching out the door with Christina. He knew he had only himself to blame for her standoffish behavior.

The hours lagged until his swim meet. He needed something to boost his energy and tried everything he had packed from home: protein shake, bottle of Gatorade, and a protein bar. Though he knew Coach Harris wouldn't approve at this late point in the season, he even purchased a candy bar from the vending machine. Still, nothing worked. How could it, when so many thoughts burdened his mind?

At the pool, even the excitement of his teammates and the smell of fresh-baked chocolate chip cookies rising over the scent of chlorine couldn't boost his low energy levels. He went through his regular routine of stretching, then dipping his swim cap in the water and dumping it over his head. The water tingled in contact with his skin, but nothing more. He fixed his goggles in position and tried to clear the clutter in his mind, hoping the act would calm his nerves. He tried to imagine entering the pool and visualizing the colors a normal person would see.

Without glancing at the stands or Coach Harris, he stepped up onto the blocks for the announcer to begin the two hundred individual medley. He bent down to grasp the starting block. Before the buzzer sounded, the swimmer next to him exploded off the blocks.

Casey's body instinctively reacted, ready to spring when logic struck. In milliseconds, he realized everyone else still waited for the official start. With taut muscles, he fiercely grabbed the blocks and teetered forward but successfully prevented his dive.

His heart raced as a shot of adrenaline flooded his veins, instantly revitalizing him like he had injected a dose of caffeine directly into his nervous system. His arms felt jerky, his flexed calf muscles twitched spasmodically, and his brain kicked into high alert, knowing a false start would disqualify him from the race.

The race announcer permitted them to come off the blocks while the swimmer who false started returned to the side of the pool. The boy slammed his fist against the water with frustration, then exited the pool, swearing under his breath for getting himself disqualified before the race had even begun.

Casey stepped down from his starting block, hoping to ground himself once the cool, wet tiles sat beneath his feet once more. He stretched his shoulders, arms, and legs, trying to refocus. He jumped up and down three times, then took a deep breath and exhaled slowly. "Get it together," he scolded himself. "You can do this."

The race announcer signaled for them to step onto the blocks once more. Casey tried to ignore the empty lane next to him, focusing his exhausted mind on the race instead. He took his position, ready to explode off the block at the sound of the buzzer.

The water bubbles prickled the sides of his body as he entered the water. His eyes trained on the favorable colors of water as he instinctively propelled himself forward with his feet locked together in a swift dolphin kick. Yet his arms felt like lead when they broke the water in the butterfly. His stroke turned robotic, and Casey imagined himself in automaton mode, swimming without heart.

Eight lengths later, he slammed his hand into the touchpad at the end of his freestyle sprint. He removed the goggles from his eyes and glanced over at Coach Harris.

Despite finishing first, Coach Harris shook his head with dismay at Casey's lackluster performance. Casey looked up at his time on the scoreboard. It was good enough to break the old record but not nearly as impressive as the one he had just set two meets ago. And this close to Sections, his coach expected him to improve in every race.

Mandi stopped by his lane as he climbed out of the water. Casey immediately noticed the lack of bounce to her step. "Congrats on taking first, but there's not a lot I can do with this since your main competition had false started," she admitted. "Any chance you want to go into how you can 'read the water'?" Her chocolate brown eyes focused on him with a pleading look.

Casey shook his head. Describing the synesthesia for the entire student body to read would have been embarrassing enough. Now to learn his abilities came from a different source entirely made it impossible to mention. "Not really," he apologized.

"Maybe some other time," she said, a hint of hope written across her face.

"Maybe," Casey replied, knowing deep in his heart he would never reveal that secret. He walked away to join his team on the bench.

"That was an ugly win," Coach Harris told Casey. "Your stroke seemed a little off."

"You're right, Coach. I'll do better next time," Casey said, learning long ago that his coach didn't tolerate excuses.

"I hope so. You've come so far to blow it at the last minute," he said bluntly.

Casey swallowed hard, knowing every word held the obvious truth. "Yes, Coach."

He gave Casey an encouraging slap across his shoulder. "Well, pull it together. We've got a few big weeks ahead of us."

Casey allowed himself a small sigh of relief. At least his coach hadn't given up on him entirely. "A few big weeks" meant he still expected Casey to come through and make it past States. If he could pull everything together, and after all he'd learned recently, that might be a pretty big "if."

Casey steeled his weary mind. He wouldn't let his coach down. But he had to figure a few things out in advance, and he suddenly knew exactly where to begin.

CHAPTER TWELVE

After the meet, Casey dropped off his mom at home and headed over to Great Plains High School, hoping to catch Owen Teague after he'd finished with his own swim meet. He only had to wait a few minutes before Owen exited the pool's locker room, his attention focused on his phone and his characteristic orangey haze rising like steam off the bit of damp hair that protruded from under his black hood. Casey walked right up to Owen, not caring that he startled him with his rapid approach. He pointed an accusatory finger right at Owen's chest, snipping, "I had a good thing going until you starting messing with my head."

"It's nice to see you, too," Owen retorted with a heap of sarcasm. His hazel eyes narrowed as his lips shifted into a scowl. He spoke sharply in his own defense. "Look, man, I only stated the obvious that, quite honestly, I thought you already knew. Besides, you've got nothing to gripe about. I just moved here from Phoenix, and let me tell you something: your weather here sucks." He pulled a winter hat from his pocket and angrily stuffed it onto his head, snuffing out the wisps of orange steam.

Casey opened his mouth to speak, then shut it again, at a

loss for words.

"Listen, dude. For all it's worth, I'm sorry," Owen added in a softer tone. "I remember how I felt like crap when I first found out."

Casey's eyebrows perched high on his forehead. "You did?"

Owen nodded. His gaze shifted, looking at nothing in particular as if lost in remembrance of that event.

"Can you tell me about it? 'Cause I'm still having a hard time with this whole thing," Casey admitted.

"Take a seat," Owen suggested, gesturing to a set of student benches down the hall. "It's not a short story."

Together they walked far from the locker room door and any athletes lingering after practice. Casey followed Owen's lead and sat down.

"I first learned about my abilities when I was very young... at my grandfather's funeral. My grandpa was a respected firefighter in the community, until one day he didn't make it back to the station." Owen paused and exhaled deeply. "I guess I was so upset that I didn't realize what was going on. My parents gave me a candle to hold during his vigil, and I didn't seem to notice anything was wrong, but the next thing I knew, everyone was staring at me, their mouths opened wide in surprise. Apparently, I was holding the candle for so long that the hot wax had dripped down the side and right onto my small fingers. I didn't flinch — didn't even notice, for that matter. How could I? Grandpa had been like a second father to me, and then all of a sudden, he was gone. Afterwards, my distant relatives gave my parents their condolences and patted me on the head as consolation. Each one asked if I wanted to be a fireman like my grandfather." Owen scowled at the memory. "I despised their patronizing tones."

"Was your grandpa a fire elly, too?" Casey wondered. It would make sense if that originally drew him to his career.

"He was, but he died in a backdraft. Do you know what

that is?"

Casey shook his head.

"It was horrible. Absolutely horrible." Owen clasped his hands together in a tight squeeze, his skin pulled taut over white knuckles. He swallowed hard before elaborating. "Sometimes in a burning building, the fire will burn until all the oxygen is depleted in a room. Only it becomes very dangerous at this point because the hot gases and fuels in the air still remain in high concentrations. If the windows in the building are closed, there's not enough ventilation in the room for the gases to escape, and there's not enough oxygen left to combust. So it's like everything waits until just the right conditions come up again...and that's exactly what happened when my grandpa broke open the door."

Casey's eyes widened. "What happened? When the conditions were right, I mean?"

Owen sighed, digging his hands deep into the pocket of his black hoodie. "As soon as he broke down the door to that enclosed room, oxygen reentered the area and ignited all the hot gases and fuels that hadn't completely burned. Essentially, the whole room suddenly combusted, causing a backdraft, and massive flames shot out the opening, and Grandpa was caught right in the middle of it," Owen finished. His lips drew into a solemn frown.

"I'm so sorry," Casey said, though he knew his words couldn't erase Owen's pain. His blue eyes left Owen's face and respectfully shifted down toward the floor instead.

Owen shook his head sadly like he still couldn't believe the tragedy had occurred. "He could save everyone else. But even with his so-called 'powers,' he couldn't save himself. I wanted nothing to do with that career. Nothing to do with fire at all, for that matter. So I decided to try something totally different. And you know what? It turns out fire and water aren't so incompatible after all." He finished with a small chuckle.

"What do you mean?" Casey wondered, lifting his head

with curiosity.

Owen admitted, "I used to be strong-willed—sometimes pig-headed, I suppose."

Casey was about to say, "How is that any different than now?" but held his tongue. He didn't know Owen well enough to roast him. Not yet, at least.

"Eventually, I became pretty rebellious, and fought out against my parents' claims. I actually took up swimming on purpose. I guess you could say it was out of spite for them all." Owen's chuckle turned into a deep-throated laugh. "I know, it's not what you'd expect from a fire elly, but I learned to fuel my anger into improving my stroke, just to prove everybody was wrong about me. But what I didn't realize was I had started out in swimming for all the wrong reasons. I thought I could show them I was right, and to rebel against everything associated with fire ellies.

"Funny thing was, eventually I started to race for myself and my grandpa's honor instead. I learned to use my fire powers to warm myself up before races. That's why I sit there with my headphones on. By separating myself from all the activity ahead of time, I can concentrate on changing my body's temperature. I soon found that the temperature of my body could affect the density of water surrounding me, so I learned to use it to create less resistance."

"Wow," Casey said with a low whistle of amazement. That sure seemed to beat his ability to read the colors of the water to find the best path of travel, away from the interference with swimmers in adjacent lanes. In Owen's case, he didn't just see the best path, he *created* it.

"Plus, I've found it can help out a whole lot here in the winter." He gave a shiver for effect. "I know my blood was thin from living down in the desert, but still. How can you people stand it around here? It feels like freaking forty below every day!"

Casey snorted. Before he raced Owen, he had interpreted

his aloof and disengaged behavior as posing no threat, when in reality it was the complete opposite. Owen intentionally used that time to mentally prepare himself for the upcoming event in a way Casey could never have imagined.

"I remember I got in trouble a few times for 'playing with fire.' Neither of my parents showed the trait; they claimed it had skipped a generation. But they were worried about me. It wasn't my fault," Owen continued. "The kid was a jerk and didn't stop picking on me. I guess he didn't expect me to fight back. Not in that way, at least."

"What happened?" Casey wondered.

"He told everyone I had a lighter and set the bench out on the playground on fire, but it wasn't like that. You know how sometimes the feeling inside gets so bad you can't control it?" Owen asked, his hazel eyes gauging Casey for a sign of confirmation.

Only Casey shook his head. He couldn't remember ever feeling that way. Except maybe that might explain what happened when he spilled blue paint over Taylor's white jersey.

"The kid said I had a contraband lighter at school, but the truth was I didn't even know how to use one. I was only seven years old, for God's sake. They searched me and found nothing, of course, except everyone believed him since it was the only logical explanation. After that incident, the kids at school called me a pyro. I even had to meet with a juvey officer for a bit to make sure I was mentally stable. My parents thought I had been through enough, so they decided to move. We kept moving every few years. I guess it was their way of trying to help."

"Did you get in trouble again? Is that why you're here?"

Owen shrugged. "Nah. This time they said they got tired of the heat. Maybe they thought I needed a full break from the desert, like the area was too tempting. So they decided to make a complete change and bring me to the Land of 10,000 Lakes, like that could contain me. Fat chance of worrying about that now;

not when it's so stinking cold outside."

"At least you've got a built-in thermostat," Casey joked.

"Thank God for that," Owen agreed.

* * * *

Even after his conversation with Owen, the issue continued to dwell in Casey's mind. Owen hinted at a biological connection, passed down from his grandfather. Grandma Louise had told him the same thing, that she possessed the ability, as did his father, Hugh. If only he could talk to Hugh to find out more. A trip up north seemed the only way to resolve the confusion that corrupted his every waking thought and manipulated his dreams at night.

There might be one other person who could help. Casey guessed it was too late to call, but at least Taylor would get his text in the morning.

He typed, *Question for you.*

Surprisingly, she was still up and got back to him in a matter of seconds.

Shoot.

Is anyone else in your family also an ice "e"? He was careful not to write out the word "elly" like she had warned.

Still dwelling on this?

He could practically hear her laughter ringing in his ear. *Idk.* Then he shook his head, reconsidering his response. *Yeah. Pretty much.*

Taylor typed back, *My dad played hockey in college, and my mom was a figure skater.*

Just as Casey had suspected.

I need to know more, so I'm going to find my father.

When R U going?

This weekend. Can't wait any longer.

I'm free. Want me to come for support?

She obviously didn't realize his father lived up north. Either that, or she was really bored. Though it was nice of her to volunteer to help, Casey simply couldn't accept her offer. He needed to take care of this on his own.

CHAPTER THIRTEEN

"Mom, I've been thinking," Casey began, catching his mother in their sunny yellow kitchen on Wednesday after practice. He had rehearsed his plan over and over again in his head but strangely felt at a loss for words once the opportunity arose to actually voice his intent. "Can I, um, borrow the car this weekend to go and visit Hugh?"

She gasped. "Your dad?"

Casey nodded. He had always called him either "Hugh Donnelly" or his "father." In Casey's mind, the title of "Dad" wasn't given but earned. Hugh might be his biological father, but he'd done nothing to deserve Casey calling him anything else.

"Now? But you've got Sections and States coming up!" his mom objected, her voice rising a full octave with surprise.

"You didn't have a problem with it last weekend when you sent me to Grandma's," Casey reminded her.

"That was a chance for you to get away and let yourself relax. And you know what, I think my plan completely failed. Ever since you've come back, you've seemed more agitated and stressed out than ever. I don't know what's gotten into you lately, but I think you need to figure this out and fast," she advised.

"That's exactly why I need to go up there." He pulled up the extended forecast and radar on his phone to prove the weekend would be clear of winter storms. He promised to stop halfway at Grandma's and pick up Bo for companionship. He'd pack plenty of healthy snacks in the car to keep up his energy reserves during the trip. Plus, he only planned to visit Hugh for a short time, then would return to Grandma Louise's for the night, so he'd be home early on Sunday morning, giving himself plenty of time to rest and recuperate for the next week. And he promised to pull over someplace safe if he ever had to use the phone en route.

While his mom mulled this information over in her mind, Casey made a mental note to pack his paints and a canvas with him this time, just in case. That pencil drawing of the deep ocean dream continued to haunt him, and when he tried to recreate it on canvas, the color sensations didn't come out exactly as he remembered. He still planned to gift it to his grandma as a reminder of her incredible treasure, but he wanted to be prepared just in case. He had learned he couldn't reproduce the color sensations once the images had fled his mind; the impressions must be fresh in order for him to accurately express his ideas in the painting.

His thorough preparation surprised Ellen. She eventually consented with a deep, weighted sigh. "Fine. But for the record, I think this is very, very bad timing."

"I'm sorry," Casey said, his voice filled with sincerity. He placed a comforting arm over his mom's shoulders.

She shook her head. "Sometimes, it seems you're growing up too fast. I know you'll be off to college soon, and you may want to continue swimming there, so I'm trying to help you prepare. But he's your father, and I shouldn't hold it against you for wanting to see him. I'm only afraid you won't get the reaction from him that you want."

"Why do you say that?" he wondered.

"Aside from the fact that he's wanted nothing to do with you for the past fifteen years or more?" She took a deep breath. "I'm sorry. That came out a bit harsher than I intended."

Casey took a deep breath, restraining the hundreds of questions that flooded his mind, hoping she'd delve into more details than the brief story she'd repeated countless times over the years. In the past, she'd grown so upset that he eventually stopped asking. He only knew a few facts about his father, such as Hugh had left them soon after Casey was born. Casey had always suspected that his birth served as the primary reason for Hugh's hasty departure. However, this new information from Grandma Louise radically changed his mind. Casey had a sinking suspicion Hugh had based his reasons more on the newfound explanation of his water elemental powers than on a newborn's addition to the family.

"We met when I was going to college in Florida, and your father was working the show," his mom spoke, her words slow and pained. "He began skiing right out of high school."

Casey had heard this part before. She'd told him before that his father was a talented water skier and worked at the Cypress Gardens water show. Now that Casey knew he possessed water elly powers, the job seemed so much more fitting for him. He wondered if any other parts of the story would sound different in light of his understanding of ellies.

"One day, he had a really bad accident when the handle slipped out of his grasp in the middle of a stunt, making him crash into the ramp and tear the ligaments in his knee."

Casey held his breath, yearning for more. She'd never shared details beyond the accident before.

"He loved performing," she continued, her eyes holding a faraway gaze like she remembered watching his show many times.

Casey tried to imagine the water skiing show from the few

pictures he'd seen on the Internet where performers completed amazing acrobatic jumps and flips off ramps; skied barefoot backwards on one leg, seemingly hanging on to the handle of the tow rope with only their toes; and formed incredible pyramids while skiing in tandem. He envisioned the motorboat kicking up spray as it zoomed past the crowd gathered in the stands beneath a sky of blazing blue. Behind the boat, Hugh received wild cheers as he waved to the adoring crowd, then turned his skis' tips to angle himself toward the ramp, his knees like shock absorbers as he flew across the wake. Suddenly, the crowd rose to their feet and emitted a collective gasp as the towrope's handle ripped away from his grasp, dangerously bouncing and skipping across the surface of the water at high speeds. Losing control, Hugh struggled to stay upright before he slammed into the ramp, destroying his knee and shattering his dreams. For a long moment, Hugh floated in his lifejacket, his face contorted into a grimace of excruciating pain. Eventually, he mustered the strength to lift one heavy hand from the water in a half-hearted wave as the boat circled around to pick him up. The crowd clapped in polite respect, but it wasn't the same. It would never be the same again.

She shook her head. Her words snapped Casey from his reverie. "The accident seemed to steal all of the life from him. Of course, he had to quit his job and was never quite as happy afterwards, like he was filled with guilt and regret for skipping college to ski for a living."

"Why didn't he try something else besides water skiing?" he asked.

When Ellen shrugged, Casey could sense the burden she carried by holding this information inside, close to her heart, weighing down her shoulders. "I guess he didn't want to go back to college at that point in his life. Nowadays, he could've gotten a degree online, but back then, those options didn't exist. We only had brick and mortar institutions, and after being out in the real world, he refused to take a step back in time.

"For almost a year, he struggled after finding a menial paying desk job in Florida and hated every minute of it, so he convinced me to move back to his home state of Minnesota with him. I had my teaching license approved for this state and soon found a job at my middle school. I have to admit, the weather was brutally cold and took some time to get used to, but I adjusted, bought a really warm jacket and pair of boots, and eventually grew to love it here."

She placed one hand over Casey's and gave him a small squeeze. "Right before you were born, Hugh changed. It wasn't your fault, of course. I think it's more like he came to the realization that he didn't want to work nine to five at a desk job for the rest of his life, and without warning, decided to quit and move up north to manage a campground. I could tell the long commute and sitting in bumper-to-bumper traffic had started to eat away at him. He grew to become a hollow shell of his former self. Still, I couldn't believe he didn't talk to me about it beforehand. All of a sudden, that was it. I could either move with him or lose him forever."

"Yeah, but you're a teacher. You could've found a job anywhere," Casey noted.

"I love my school, but it wasn't just that. Moving up north meant colder and longer winters, fewer neighbors, and lack of convenience to shopping centers. Maybe I would've grown accustomed to it, only at the time I didn't want to have to drive a half hour or more just to get to a grocery store." She gave a wistful sigh. "I guess you could say we couldn't reach a compromise. Hugh claimed he was drawn to the water, and that's why he wanted to move. Deep down, I knew the real reason was that I didn't rank paramount in his heart...and that admission was difficult to get past." Ellen lifted her hand off Casey's to brush her light brown hair from her face, and he could see that her eyes looked glassy with fresh tears. "For a while, I thought of returning to Florida. You could've grown up in a warm climate, near the beach and plenty of sunshine."

"So why didn't you?"

"I hesitated in taking you so far away from your father," his mom explained. "I thought you'd never have the chance to get to know him as you grew up. I have to admit, I never expected that would eventually happen anyway. I thought he'd still show an interest in you, visiting you sometimes on holidays or asking for you to spend part of the summer with him, but he never did. Then, as we grew more established in this community, it became harder and harder to leave. I didn't want to pull you away from your friends at school. I would've had to apply for a whole new teaching license with no guarantee of a job down south. I know it doesn't sound like a very good reason, but it had become so much easier to stay than to start all over again." She looked off into the distance, letting her eyes drift out the kitchen window, unable to meet his gaze again.

Casey frowned. He'd forgotten about the numerous lost opportunities over the years simply because his father chose not to exist in his life. Suddenly he wondered why he was bothering to make contact with Hugh at all. He obviously didn't care about Casey, or he would have done something to show it.

"It's not like I don't enjoy going up north," she continued as if justifying her actions. "I'm all for a nice, relaxing day on the water or spending a weekend up at the cabin. But Hugh was married to his rod and reel." When she chuckled, Casey detected a trace of bitter sadness in her laugh.

* * * *

On Saturday morning, Casey stopped by Grandma Louise's house to pick up Bo for the remainder of the drive north. He made sure to bring the painting of his dream with the golden treasure chest left undiscovered in the sunken Spanish galleon, deep beneath the sea. He took another look at his work before handing it to Grandma Louise. The bold splashes of color grew increasingly darker from the top to the bottom of the canvas, not fully blended but weaving from crimson to purple to a deep navy blue, like the grass fronds of a homemade basket. Near the bottom, three black crosses tilted at extreme angles jutted from the deep, barely visibly against the deep, dark waters. Faded yellow lines radiated outward from a collection of small, golden orbs that he had applied as heavy dabs of paint and dried as textured dots. He didn't think he got the colors quite right from his pencil sketch, but it felt pretty close to what he remembered from the shockingly realistic dream. And judging by her widening smile, Casey knew she understood its intent.

"I *love* it," she said, beaming, and pulled him into a warm, one-armed hug that seemed to erase all of his uncertainties about the accuracy of his recollections. "I've got just the perfect place to hang this."

"Glad to hear it. It's been on my mind quite a bit lately."

Grandma Louise nodded and released him from her embrace. "Your mom warned me in advance that you've been having a pretty rough week, especially when you've got some big races coming up. I know it's tough, but you've got to work through this little bit of uncertainty now so you can focus your energy on your future. It's my fault, and I'm sorry to you and your mom. I never told Ellen about the existence of elementals, so she didn't understand the real reason Hugh had left. It was particularly difficult for your father. We don't exactly fit into this world the same way others do," she added. "For us water ellies, water has natural healing properties, and bathwater rejuvenates me. Why do you think I still look so young? Why I've lived so much longer than your grandfather? Or why I choose to live on a lake?" Grandma Louise noted.

"This is your lot in life. Everyone has something they must deal with. But not everyone accepts elemental powers in the same way, which can be quite dangerous. There are reasons why your dad was afraid to tell anyone. Now he lives alone on an island."

Lines of worry creased his grandmother's forehead. "I need to let you know. He may not be happy you're there."

"I figured as much. But I still need to know," Casey said, opening the passenger side door and gesturing for the dog to enter.

Bo jumped into the car, his mouth opened in a huge grin at the thrill of a car ride. He wagged his tail happily against the seat and dashboard like a beating drum as he turned around three times before plopping into the seat. "Don't worry about his supper. He can eat when he gets back home. Bo travels much better on an empty stomach, believe me." She handed Casey a foldable water dish from her pocket. "This is really all you'll need for him."

"Thanks," Casey said, placing it on the passenger's side floor mat. He turned to leave when Grandma Louise restrained him with a surprisingly firm grip on his shoulder. He stopped in his tracks, noticing the apprehension written in his grandmother's wrinkled expression and clouded, steely eyes.

"Just be careful. And be ready," she warned, then released his shoulder to let him leave.

* * * *

Be careful. Be ready. What did she mean by that particular choice of words? Casey contemplated her intention as he pulled out of the winding driveway and headed on his way, following the directions to Hugh's address at the Thousand Acres Campground that he'd already plugged into the GPS.

Be ready for what? Rejection? How would that be any different than the feelings he'd endured every day of his life? He'd learned to move on. Besides, his mom was always there for support.

Casey drove north through clear, crisp skies and the brilliant sunbeams glaring off the snow. He eventually turned off the interstate, making his way over the less groomed country roads. The car rattled over the uneven surface, and Casey felt the bumps in the dirt road under the packed snow cover like when he'd thrown his dirty shoes in the laundry machine's spin cycle. He noticed the driveways here were far too long to shovel. Instead, residents had plows attached on the front of their trucks to clear the way to the mailbox and maybe even the rest of the street, just so they could get out after a heavy snow.

Casey imagined his father's campground must be a pretty hopping place during the summer months. However, today it resembled a ghost town with heaps of snow filling the grooves of each carved letter on the wooden THOUSAND ACRES CAMPGROUND sign, making it difficult to read. Vacant campers hunkered down under deep snowbanks that blocked the front entrance to each door. Camping grills barely peeked above a thick layer of white. Owners had secured their canoes on the racks many warm months ago, more from fear of damage from high winds than theft, Casey imagined, in this desolate area.

A small office manager's cabin, built from interlocking logs with a sharp angled roof, sat at the front of the property. Two signs hung in the windows. One read BAIT SHOP, and the other, CLOSED FOR THE SEASON, but Casey knocked anyway. He patiently waited a few moments with Bo at his heel but received only silence as his reply.

He glanced out past the cabin where a dozen icehouses dotted the white expanse. A few had trucks parked nearby, right on the surface of the lake. Despite the late morning hour, he couldn't see a soul — though it didn't entirely surprise him with the biting wind and bitter temperatures outside.

Casey figured he might as well try and wandered out toward the closest icehouse. "Let's go, buddy," he said, waving Bo along. As they ventured out onto the open lake marked with a line of distant trees on the opposite shore, the wind picked up, ripping across the open space and tearing through his clothes. He instinctively squinted as protection from the blinding sun and blustery weather, his eyes beginning to water, making him wish he'd thought far enough ahead to grab the spare pair of sunglasses in the glove box. To combat the effects of the biting cold, he zippered his collar to its highest point and tucked his nose deep inside. He pulled his hat down over his ears and wedged his bare hands deep within his pockets. Soon, the faint taste of frozen peaches and strawberry lemonade popsicles filled his mouth. "That's a new one," Casey mumbled to himself, still unsure if synesthesia or his water elemental abilities accounted for the tastes that resembled the ones he'd experienced the weekend before at his grandmother's lake.

The walk across the flat frozen surface was tougher than he expected. With every step, his feet broke through a thick crust where the snow had melted, then later refroze under the sun's bright but cold and distant rays. Beneath the crust, he quickly sank into a layer of incredibly soft powder. Rather than continue with the laborious effort of blazing his own trail, he found a set of packed-down snowmobile tracks and followed those. Bo didn't seem to mind, however. He leapt animatedly through the deep snowdrifts, frolicking in his freedom out on the open lake.

Casey knocked on the door of the nearest icehouse. A man with a scraggly graying beard and thick brown eyebrows like furry caterpillars across his forehead opened the door. He wore a tan pair of lined work pants and an insulated winter jacket. His plaid earflap hat was turned up along the brim to expose a fluffy fleece layer underneath. His pale blue eyes studied Casey, but his face remained expressionless.

Casey opened his mouth to speak, then reconsidered. He detected no hint of recognition in the man's face, making him conclude this was definitely not his father. So busy with training for swimming during the winter months, Casey had never spent much time exploring outdoor winter sports. As a result, he'd never actually seen an icehouse on the inside, only towed behind trucks on trailers as outdoorsmen traveled north for the weekend. Curiosity winning the best of him, Casey peered inside past the man.

A pull string connected to a single overhead light bulb illuminated the room. Intricate webs of frosty crystals covered the perimeter of the sole window overlooking the frozen expanse of the lake. On the side of one wall sat a simple stove and a bottle of water by a makeshift sink. Casey instantly noticed the icehouse had no plumbing or heat for obvious reasons, but still, it seemed significantly warmer than outside, the shelter providing a buttress against the fierce gusts across the frozen lake. Several perfect holes drilled with an ice auger stood open at the foot of the bunk beds. From his angle, he could see the black inky water through each hole in the thick ice. He imagined you'd really have to watch where you stepped, or your leg could fall right through one of the holes.

The man crossed his arms over his chest, his lips curling into a scowl as he grew increasingly impatient.

Casey swallowed down the huge lump in his throat for disturbing the man's fishing trip. Still, he had driven most of the morning driving up here and needed his answers resolved so he could move on with his life. Before he lost his nerve, he mustered up the strength to speak. "Do you know if Hugh Donnelly is around here today?"

The man gave a loud harrumph. "That depends on who wants to know," he gruffly replied.

CHAPTER FOURTEEN

Casey took a step back, stunned by the man's demeanor and breath that reeked of bitter malt and hops with every word. Casey glanced past the man and noticed half a six-pack of beer sat on the countertop, already downed this morning.

"I'm Casey. Casey Donnelly," he said. "And this is my grandma Louise's dog, Bo," he added, scratching the golden retriever on the head.

The man blinked momentarily, his eyes skimming over Casey to fix on Bo. "Hmmf. Looks a little like the dog we had when I was a kid." Then his expression hardened, and his pale blue eyes turned steel cold. "So, what do you want?"

Casey stood a little straighter, remembering Grandma Louise's suggestion to bring Bo along to soften his temper. He paused for a few seconds before responding. "I'm looking for my father."

The man turned around and walked back into his icehouse, muttering to himself. He quickly busied himself with preparing the tackle for his fishing pole propped against the bunks.

"Are you Hugh? Are you my father?" Casey asked again,

trying to decipher the man's intentions.

"Why are you here?" he barked, deliberately dodging Casey's questions.

Casey swallowed hard. His mom and Grandma Louise had warned him that Hugh may not be happy to see him, but this definitely wasn't the welcome he had wanted. He tried to imagine shifting places with the man and having spent the past decade and a half without forming a connection with his own child. He just couldn't do it, couldn't envision not wanting to be a constant presence in his child's life. And yet, this man seemed completely ambivalent to the news of Casey's identity. Maybe he wasn't even Hugh at all.

Casey quickly weighed his options and decided to go with the direct, though discreet, choice of a reply. "I just found out I was a water elly."

"A water *what*?" the man snapped back, a hint of incredulity in his rough tone.

"A water elemental," Casey clarified, certain if this was indeed Hugh, that combination of words might elicit a harsh response. He instantly added, "And I wanted to understand more about what that means. I need to learn about my past."

The man clenched his jaw, his eyes narrowing into thin slits. "I didn't need you to remind me of who I was. And I certainly don't want you coming here and reminding me now. I spend every day of my life trying to forget about my past."

Casey took a step back, surprised by the severity of his accusations. Still, a very small part of him rejoiced in his accomplishment. After all of these years, he had definitely located his father, Hugh. "What do you mean, 'Who you were'?" he asked eagerly, desperate for more.

Hugh scowled in return, his voice dripping with repulsion. "An oddity. An aberration. It's not normal. I already saw the signs in you."

Casey's brow knitted. "What signs?" Without waiting for

the invitation he thought would never come, he took a step inside the icehouse, with Bo close behind. He removed his hand from his pocket to stroke the dog's head, finding comfort in the motion of his fingers against the smooth fur.

Hugh let out a heavy sigh, his gaze never leaving his tackle. "When you were a baby, your mom would blow on your face to get you to hold your breath. Even when you were only a couple of months old, you were perfectly at ease underwater. It's not normal to show no fear."

"So what? That can't be very unusual," Casey objected. He bet lots of babies felt at ease in the water since it couldn't feel much different than being carried in the mother's womb.

Hugh shook his head, muttering to himself in a voice too low to hear. A war seemed to rage inside of him, his face showing a range of emotions that Casey had trouble reading. "You could also hear sounds of water that others could not. You would turn toward the source of the sound — like when you were in your crib, you'd hear a water drip coming from the basement. Just so you know, that soft of a sound doesn't carry up two flights of stairs."

Casey nodded, realizing this information probably explained why he could hear the drinking fountain at school all the way down the hall or the annoying drip of a leaky faucet too far away for others to notice. "If others weren't bothered by the noise, then how did you know I heard the water?" he wondered.

"Because *I* could hear it, too," he replied. He waited a lengthy pause before continuing. "It's better that I left. You didn't need me. You were better off with your mom."

"So I could figure things out on my own?" Casey's voice gained an octave as frustration began to build in his blood.

"Go away," Hugh said coldly. He dropped his bait and line, not caring that the bobber bounced across the icy floor and dropped into one of the open holes. Hugh staggered on his feet, whether from anger or inebriation, Casey couldn't decide. His eyes glazed over, appearing to lose focus, then rolled back into his head, showing only the eerie whites. His cheek muscles clenched, twitching spasmodically. Then his arms left his sides, rising toward the ceiling of the icehouse, his palms facing upward. "GO AWAY!" he shouted, loud enough for anyone in the icehouses or along the shore to hear.

Casey stared at him, frightened and unnerved by Hugh's peculiar actions. Before he had time to comprehend their meanings, sudden changes around him battled for his attention. A strange gurgling sound filled the air, growing louder in intensity. Casey's eyes widened, searching for the source. He noticed the blackened water began to bubble inside each of the holes cut out of the ice with the auger tool, making the red and white plastic bobber rock violently like riding the waves on the stormy sea. Bo stood at attention on all fours, his tail poised straight behind him with alertness, and gave a series of short, alarmed barks at the water's odd behavior.

Casey suspected Hugh's powers grew when his temper flared into an uncontrollable rage, presumably augmented by the effects of alcohol. "Bo, let's go," he whispered, placing one hand on the dog's collar and backing out of the door.

They'd made it a few steps onto the open ice when dark water jettisoned simultaneously out of the holes in the floor like the mouth of a fire hose turned on high. The blasts rocketed against the roof of the icehouse, shattering the bare lightbulb with a barrage of sparks. Unable to withstand the mounting pressure, the floor near the holes began to crack and cave inward, leaving a huge gaping hole of exposed water in the middle of the floor of the icehouse.

"C'mon, Bo!" Casey screamed, his eyes growing wide as he turned on his heels. With the dog at his side, they fled across the frozen lake, their progress hindered by the uneven snow cover. Casey snuck a glance over his shoulder and saw streams of water pierce the roof of the icehouse like the full blast of a fire hose. As they ran faster, Casey feared the ice under his own feet would soon give way, dropping him into the deadly cold water lying beneath its surface.

Behind him, Casey heard Hugh utter a deafening cry of defeat. Casey's foot caught on an edge of crusted snow, making him trip and scrape his knees and hands across the jagged, granular surface. His jeans took the brunt of the blow against his knees, but his bare palms burned as the crystallized snow lacerated his skin. He looked with dismay at the bright red blood leaking from his fresh cuts. His hands throbbed when the bitter cold made contact with his open wounds. His pain quickly fled from his thoughts as an ominous cleaving sound from the direction of the icehouse reminded him he had bigger concerns to worry about.

Casey turned and saw the lake ice around the structure break up, and the icehouse walls start to submerge, quickly engulfed in the dark open water. Had the water responded to Hugh's request? Was this the power his father exhibited as a water elemental? Hugh now stood alone on a solitary slab of ice, appearing to command the deadly cold waters that surrounded him.

The inky water bubbled into a frenzy, fueled with an intense power growing beneath Hugh's form. With a resounding crack, the ice encircling the open water buckled from the buildup of water pressure beneath. Fissures littered the surface like glacial crevasses, creaking and groaning as if expressing great discomfort. Large slabs of ice buckled like fallen stacks of giant dominoes.

Hugh's latent anger frightened Casey. All these years, Casey had thought his synesthesia seemed unusual, so he purposefully distanced himself from others and kept his secret to himself. But he'd learned to use the condition to his advantage. Only Casey knew about the colors he saw in the water, and only he understood the true meanings behind his paintings. His abilities never posed a physical threat to anyone.

Yet here on the lake, Hugh's fury endangered many people's lives. The ice fishermen didn't expect the lake ice to break up this early in the season. Would they be able to escape in time? Casey hoped they had heeded Hugh's warning before their own houses and trucks slipped into the lake. In fact, he wasn't sure even he and Bo would reach the safety of the shore.

"I should have accepted Taylor's offer to come out here with me," Casey lamented. "This is totally her element."

The intense brightness of the midday sun's reflection off the snow blinded him. He couldn't discern any variations across its surface until the danger loomed too close. Knowing he couldn't trust his vision to help, Casey listened to the sound of breaking glass as the hunks and shards of ice piled up behind him, carried forth on the crest of the incoming wave. His annoying talent of detecting the sound of water at incredible distances had always seemed a distraction in the past. He found it particularly irritating when someone stopped at the water fountain down the hall, especially in the middle of his exams. The gurgling fountain rang in his ears, upsetting his concentration. Worse, the delicious taste of hot apple pie topped with whipped cream would pervade his mouth, making his stomach twist with hunger, even if he'd just finished lunch. The lunch ladies never served any desserts like that in the cafeteria.

Yet today, he found a new purpose for this heightened sense. Casey could feel the water prickle inside his skin, just like his mom's story of the water witches and dowsers in drought-stricken California. For a brief second, he closed his eyes. He felt a trickle of water brush against his arm hair, heightening his senses. When he reopened his eyes, he saw his father standing alone on an undisturbed sheet of ice, a reddened current of dark water driving outward from his spot. Huge piles of crackling ice moved forward, carried on the cusp of the incoming wave.

Casey struggled to keep his footing on the uneven moving flow. Twice his boots slipped through the loose ice, soaking his jeans up to his knees. Each time, he managed to wedge his foot out of the pockets in the ice and search for larger pieces to support his weight, like surfing on boards fashioned from blocks of ice as the flow moved toward land.

The wave pushed forward, chunks of ice riding its crest as it swallowed up the trees that lined the shore, barreling over and snapping the trunks of the smaller saplings or parting around the massive trunks and ripping off large sections of rough bark, like peeling the skin off an orange. It pressed onward, splintering the painted siding and breaking through the boathouse window with a loud shatter of splintering glass. The wave of broken ice soon spilled through the hole it created until the entire room was filled from the floor to the ceiling. Nothing could stop its destructive force. "Be careful, Bo," he warned, watching the dog spring from one flattened chunk of ice to another as the wave overtook them.

As Casey hurriedly treaded over the uneven moving pieces, a new thought jumped to mind. After seeing the magnitude of his father's power firsthand, Casey envisioned the unfair advantage over his competition he had wielded in the pool all of these years. Deep inside his gut, something didn't feel right. How could he continue with his sport when the deception ate away at his conscience and his soul? Now that he had realized it wasn't synesthesia but his elemental abilities that lay at the root of his ability to read the water, he wondered if he had only scratched the surface of his potential. Like his father, did he have the means to unleash this deadly force?

If so, he wanted nothing to do with his connection to the water. Nothing at all. Casey figured the only way to protect himself from the destructive power he contained inside was to renounce it. He would have to abandon everything associated with water, even if that meant giving up the sport he loved.

Hugh might have been drawn to the water like his mother claimed, but at that moment, Casey chose to avoid it altogether. He would eventually move to the mountains or the desert if needed.

Anything to ensure he would not end up like his destructive father, consumed with an uncontrollable fury.

The flow began to diminish in speed when it reached the deep snowbanks near the road. Casey leapt off the chunks of ice, extremely grateful to feel the solid ground beneath his feet once more. "Bo!" he called, and the dog instantly bounded up along his side. Wet fur matted three of his paws where he had also fallen through into the water. Luckily, they had both escaped without significant damage. Casey wiped his bloodied palms against his jeans, then felt around in his pocket for the car keys. He sped toward his mom's car with Bo keeping pace. "Let's get outta here," he told the dog, eager to leave.

When they reached the driveway, Casey's feet ground to a stop. Hugh Donnelly stood in front of the hood of the car, his arms crossed over his chest in waiting.

"What were you thinking?!" Casey gasped, his mouth gaping wide. "You could have killed us! Not to mention all the others ice fishing on the lake. Their icehouses and trucks could've been destroyed...just like your icehouse...and your boathouse...." Casey fumed, his bloodied palms clenched into fists. His chest heaved with the combination of adrenaline from his narrow escape and outright anger at his father pumping through his blood.

Hugh sighed and gazed across the lake to survey his damage. "Not one of my proudest moments," he admitted, then hung his head with dismay.

Casey blinked, stunned by the utter defeat in Hugh's expression. He pushed the rest of the thoughts he had intended to shout at his father for his years of disinterest and neglect to the back of his mind. Slowly, his fists uncurled, and the boiling blood began to simmer as he realized Hugh felt sincere remorse for letting his actions slip out of his control.

And now his father stood here before him. Casey had the chance to get the answers he craved if he asked the questions in the right way to prevent Hugh from unleashing another bout of rage.

Casey swallowed, then tried a different approach. "But how did you get here? Last I saw, you were on a piece of ice in the middle of the lake, and now…?" He couldn't fathom how his father could have possibly made it back to shore before them, especially when he and Bo had gotten a head start.

Hugh remained quiet for a while, his eyes trained on the ground before he responded. "Some are called to the sea. You know, like those deep-sea fishermen. They spend most of their lives out on the water, waiting for the next big catch to provide for their landlocked families. I was called here," he explained in a surprisingly even tone. "Sometimes, the water does my bidding."

"It's still not fair. You could have taught me to use my abilities, not waited for me to find out from someone else. It was your responsibility. And instead, you left." Casey's voice sounded about as icy as his body felt, shivering in the stiff breeze. His soggy jeans had already frozen solid from the knees down. When the wind ripped across his face, each tooth root iced up all the way to the core. He sealed his lips together to buffer his teeth from the external air. Still, his efforts could not silence their chatter.

His father's pale eyes considered him with unexpected compassion. "Maybe we can still work things out. But first, let's get you out of the cold."

* * * *

"It seems like I've made a huge mess of things today. We haven't had an ice heave here in almost a decade," Hugh Donnelly said with a weighted sigh. "I can't believe I lost my icehouse and my boathouse this time."

Casey didn't know what to say. He didn't understand how anyone could possess so much anger inside that they would unintentionally wreak havoc of the magnitude Hugh had achieved across the frozen lake.

Hugh handed Casey a steaming mug of creamy hot chocolate mixed with warm milk. "Sorry, I don't have any marshmallows," he apologized.

Casey sat at the small wooden table, wrapped up in a thick fleece blanket. First aid ointment and several Band-Aids covered his abraded palms. He blew across the surface of his mug and took a small sip. "It's really good just as it is, thanks."

Hugh looked at him with skepticism. He walked across the floor of his modest cabin and threw another log on the fire. "Are you sure you're warm enough?"

Casey nodded. His pants had thawed and started to dry out.

"The fish don't ask questions," Hugh explained, his voice softer, almost defeated now. "They don't judge me because I'm different."

"I'm not judging you, either. I only wanted to know why you left," Casey amended, careful to avoid riling his anger once more. Bo lay coiled at his feet. He was glad to keep the dog close in case they had to make a hasty exit.

Hugh shrugged his shoulders and trained his eyes on a spot on the wall just above Casey's head. "I didn't fit in. You were much better off with your mom, anyway." Casey noticed that his father couldn't meet him in the eye like his excuse sounded more shallow and irresponsible than the day he had first convinced himself that was a suitable reason to leave.

"It's not fair," Casey objected. "You never even gave me a chance to get to know you. You never once bothered to tell me about our family history. Instead, I found out from some fire elly I just met." Casey felt the hairs on the back of his neck stand on end.

Despite Casey's attempts to avoid provoking his father further, Hugh's voice took on a defensive tone. "How do you think I felt? Your grandmother dumped this on me right before you were born. It wasn't like I had had any idea, either. She never once tried to tell me that perhaps my abilities had a little to do with my success at the show. Not once, until long after my career had ended. How do you think I felt?"

"Probably about as lousy as I did when I found out." Bo rested his heavy head across Casey's feet like the dog could inherently sense his frustration.

Hugh opened his mouth to protest, then shut it again without saying a word. Casey knew he had hit home with that last comment. Maybe now his father realized they had more in common than he had previously expected.

A small smile flickered across Hugh's face. "Y'know, we're always looking for a good lifeguard up here in the summer. I heard about what you did for your cousin and just thought... maybe...."

Casey sensed his dad's awkward pause. "You heard about that?" he asked, stunned. He buried the mounting anger and frustration inside of him. Wouldn't that news have provided his father a perfectly valid opportunity to have the discussion of water elementals over six years ago? Instead, Casey let the other side of him prevail: his father had cared enough to remember one important event in Casey's life, and in his own awkward sort of way, congratulated him on the accomplishment. Casey decided it best to simply take whatever praise he could get from this man and expect nothing more.

When Casey thought longer about Hugh's comment, he realized his father had offered — for the first time ever — to spend time together, something Casey had dreamed about for as long as he could remember. He thought of the summers he had spent watching other boys play catch with their dads at the park, switching from baseball to football with the change of seasons. When he was young, he had found it increasingly difficult to watch. Eventually, he avoided going to the park altogether.

He considered Hugh's suggestion for a long while. If he committed to lifeguarding up north, that meant he'd have to leave Mom alone for the summer and back out of his regular summer job coaching swim team and teaching lessons at the local pool. Even if he didn't wish to compete himself, he could at least earn money helping other youth advance in the sport.

His thoughts suddenly drifted to Taylor. She had willingly offered to come up north with him. Could she possibly like him for more than satiating her desire to vent? Was he really willing to give all of that up just because his father *finally* wished to spend some time with him? Granted, the idea tempted him, but not enough to sacrifice everything else.

"I've already got plans," Casey apologized.

"I understand." Hugh coughed and quickly diverted his gaze. Casey wondered if he used the cough as a way to mask the hint of dejection in his voice. He had to say something.

"But maybe I could come up for a weekend or something instead," Casey suggested.

Hugh turned his head toward him again. His lips turned up in a genuine smile this time. "I'd like that," he admitted.

"Me, too...Dad," Casey replied, selecting to utter that particular choice of words for the first time in his life.

CHAPTER FIFTEEN

Bo bounded out of the car as soon as Casey opened the door in front of Grandma Louise's lakeside cabin. The trip back to her home took far less time than the journey up that morning: partially due to the flood of adrenaline that shocked his system into high alertness as he relived the horrific scenes of trying to escape Hugh's ice tsunami, and partially due to the prospect of starting the father-son relationship he'd dreamed about for almost his entire existence. He felt like the trip had proven more successful than he possibly could have imagined—aside from the destroyed icehouse and boathouse, his scraped palms, and freezing wet feet, of course. Still, he was unsure if his grandmother and mom would concur, especially when they found out what he had decided for the future of his swimming career.

Even in the fading light of the winter's early setting sun, he noticed the kitchen curtains part briefly when Grandma Louise peeked out the window. He noticed she followed his every move with wary eyes from her warm spot. When he reached the front door, she opened it and quickly ushered him inside.

"So, how did it go?" she asked after closing the front door, sealing off the house from the frigid temperatures that marked the onset of a lengthy, bitter winter night.

"Do you want the long story or the short story?" he wondered aloud.

"Whichever you feel like sharing. I'm all ears." She sat him down at the kitchen table, in front of a plate of fresh oatmeal raisin cookies, then took the seat opposite him. "Oh, and you should know I found the perfect place for your latest painting… in the basement, right above the fireplace mantle."

Casey nodded as Bo wedged himself between the chairs to find a comfy spot under the table. He curled up, using Casey's feet as a pillow, and fell fast asleep. That location for the painting seemed like a very appropriate spot, right where she had first shown him the coin. He wished he could give an enthusiastic reply, but his body felt sluggish and his limbs heavy, burdened with emotion. He rested his elbows on the table, trying to figure out how to begin.

She pushed the plate of cookies toward him and held her breath, her grayish-blue eyes watching him intently, waiting for his news with rapt attention.

Though he hadn't eaten in hours, the thought of food simply didn't appeal to him until he could clear his chest and let his thoughts spill freely. "I'm thinking of quitting."

Grandma Louise stared at him, blinking once. "Quitting what?" she asked.

"Swimming. I saw what my father could do, and even though I don't have those same abilities, I do have an unfair advantage in the pool. It's not right or fair. I feel like a cheat." He let his head drop into his hands, feeling a huge weight release from his shoulders after his admission.

Her thin silver eyebrows narrowed with alarming concern. "What did he do to you?" she dared.

Casey told her about the power of the water used to break apart the lake ice and drive it against the shore, crashing into trees and houses in his fit of anger. "I don't want to be like that. I don't ever want to lose control like he did."

"Then don't," she said matter-of-factly.

"But it doesn't seem right. I'm not starting on the same foot as everyone else. I'm different, yet I'm judged under the same criteria. Worse, it doesn't *feel* right. Like everything I've worked for all these years is based on a lie. I wish you would've told me sooner. Then maybe I wouldn't have made the mistake of going into swimming in the first place." He ended with a heavy sigh, thinking of all the years he had devoted to the sport, the countless hours spent at practices and meets, swimming lap after lap in the pool.

"But why? You've been doing so well on your swim team," Grandma Louise protested. "Besides, you're smart. You've chosen to use your powers for good. Sometimes possessing these powers can seem a temptation that brings out the worst in human nature. Some elementals become obsessed with wealth, power, and fame. But you…you're not at all like that."

Casey sulked. "But I still used it for personal gain," he admitted, the knowledge sinking into his gut like a lead weight.

"Is that what you think this is about?" she exclaimed. "Your chance at future scholarships?" She gave her head an adamant shake, letting the silver curls bob around her ears. "If someone asks you to swim for their college, then you should. You would have *earned* that privilege through your own hard work and dedication. No one would come up to you and hand you a scholarship for being lazy. You're a fool if you think this is the time to throw it all away."

"You really think so?" he wondered aloud. He lifted his face to study hers. She radiated confidence and encouragement, and most of all, absolute sincerity.

"Every word," she said, her wrinkled mouth turning up into a comforting smile. "And your cousin…. Remember that summer back in the Carolinas? You saved him from being dragged out to sea. He would've *drowned* if you hadn't been there," she reminded him.

"I guess you're right," Casey agreed, thinking back to the first time when his powers had manifested themselves. But there was more to it than that. The bystanders on the beach had seen it too…he shouldn't have been able to swim that far back to shore, not in those surf conditions following the storm. And definitely not while carrying his older cousin.

"You have a gift, a natural talent," she continued, "just like they say. That's all true. You are an elite, gifted athlete. Now you feel like all those years of hard work and effort have been compromised with one solemn truth. You sit here poised on the brink of your highest level of competition, and this new revelation threatens to undermine your years of hard work, effort, and sacrifice. More surprising…you have learned that you are not alone.

"I know this secret may have come as quite the shock to you, but you need to be truthful and honest with yourself. *You aren't living a lie.* You still have a shot at making it to the Olympic Trials. And you can't just walk away from your dreams now. Do you think you haven't worked hard? Or that you haven't made sacrifices for your achievements?"

Casey nodded. "Of course I have."

"Everyone is blessed with some innate gift: size, speed, strength, intelligence. You're smart. You simply happened to find a sport that complements your elemental powers—and there's nothing wrong with that," she told him, crossing her arms over her chest to prove her point.

Casey thought about her comments for a moment. "So you're positive I'm not cheating."

"Absolutely. Seeing colors in the pool isn't a superhero trait as far as I'm concerned. Most likely, no one would even believe you. An ability like yours lies so far beyond the range of normal expectations. I truly believe that you, my dear, have nothing to worry about. If you ask me, I think you should proceed with your swimming career completely guilt free."

He considered her message for a while. Feeling the heavy weight release from his gut, he reached for a cookie from the plate and nibbled a bite off its edge. The sugary oats and plump raisins seemed to help rejuvenate his fatigued body, one of the aftereffects of the adrenaline surge during Hugh's ice heave, he figured. He took a second bite and swallowed hard before asking, "Can you see different colors in the water like I can?"

Grandma Louise shook her head. "That's one of the reasons I love your paintings so much," she said, gesturing around the kitchen at the canvases she'd hung on the walls. "I wish I could see the water as you do. These paintings let me feel like I can."

"Well, if you don't see different colors, can you show me what you can do with your powers? I mean, I know you can hold your breath a long time, but what else can you do with water?"

"My powers?" she laughed. "Casey, I'm afraid I haven't used them in decades. I wouldn't even know where to start anymore."

"Please, Grandma. The coin wasn't enough. I want to see more."

"How about we make a deal. I'll brush up on some of my old tricks, and the next time you see me, you can tell me how your race at the Olympic Trials went," she bartered with a small grin.

"But I haven't qualified even for States yet," he objected.

Her smile widened. "Oh, but you will. I firmly believe that. So promise me this; when you step out of that pool, you need to be sure you didn't hold back, and you gave it your all. You need to finish that race with no regrets. Regardless of your time or your place, then and only then, you'll know you've won."

Casey blinked, letting her advice sink in.

"And after that point, I want you to tell me all about it. What do you say?" She stuck out her hand for him to seal the deal.

Casey shook her hand. "I promise," he said, squaring his shoulders as his confidence returned.

Grandma Louise's eyes shone with a glaze of pride. Suddenly, she sat up straighter, her focus shifting over his head and out the gap between the curtains. She gasped and pointed out the window, announcing with an excited tone, "It's a special night tonight."

Casey's brow furrowed. "Why's that?"

She got up from her chair and drew back the curtain. "Take a look."

When Casey spun around in his chair to peek outside, his mouth fell open with awe. Vibrant ribbons of light green danced across the sky, pulled upward by some invisible force. The bands of green flowed across the velvety sky, blanketing the pinpricks of light with what Casey thought resembled a magical glow. He hadn't realized they had talked so long that the twilight had descended into deep, cold darkness.

"I've never seen the Northern Lights before," he admitted, unable to take his eyes off nature's beautiful display in the crisp, clear wintry night.

"It's hard to see where you live. You have too much light pollution, even in the suburbs. But out here where we're far away from city lights, every now and then they will appear."

They watched together in silence for a long while, reminding him of the late summer evenings spent on the porch, gazing across the glassy lake while they listened to nature's orchestra rising through the balmy air.

Casey finally spoke. "Grandma, do you think I might be able to take your coin with me this time?"

She smiled and pulled the plain old wooden box from the front pocket of her sweater.

He tilted his head sideways with confusion. "You've been carrying it with you since the last time I was here?"

"No, only tonight," she said, walking over to him to wrap one arm around his shoulders in a sideways hug. "I thought you might change your mind now that you're a believer."

* * * *

After a solid dinner and a hot shower, Casey dropped to sleep in an instant, his mind and body exhausted from the day's events. Soon after he closed his eyes, his body gave a rapid jerk and his skin prickled with urgency. The sweet taste of juicy peaches and chilled strawberry lemonade filled his mouth. He instinctively puckered his lips at the lemons' residual tartness. Suddenly, he felt the ground shift beneath him. He watched in helpless horror as his bed rested upon the white frozen lake. He threw his bare feet over the edge of the mattress just as the solid surface of the lake gave way beneath his feet and exposed patches of frigid open water. Before he could react, a swift current propelled him forward on an unsteady wave of crackling glass shards. He stretched his arms to the side for balance, afraid of falling into the deadly cold.

Casey's feet jockeyed for position, desperately trying to stay atop the moving mass of uneven ice chunks. He replanted his feet countless times, careful to avoid entrapment in the wedges of ice. He snuck a quick glance out of his periphery, quickly searching the lake's jumbled surface for a sign of Bo, but he couldn't see the retriever anywhere. Casey hoped the dog had already sought shelter from the destructive power.

A blast of biting wind ripped across the lake, making Casey's teeth chatter uncontrollably and freezing them instantly to the roots. He looked ahead, seeking a convenient place to leap off the heaving ice, but could not escape. The noise of broken glass rose to deafening levels when the icy wave carried him toward shore and made contact with the beach. The wave pushed forward across the snow-covered lawn, directly toward the lakefront cabin. Only it didn't stop there. The well-constructed walls provided little match for the power of a cresting frozen tsunami. Barreling on, it shattered the glass windowpanes and cascaded into the rooms, filling the entire house with a huge river of ice. Casey slipped down the jagged icy slide and landed directly on his bed, buried beneath the intrusive wave.

Shivering with fright, Casey's eyes flew open. He expected to find an alien mass of white blocks spilling through the window and littering the room with chunks of icy debris from the floor to the ceiling. Instead, the room had miraculously returned to its normal state. He blinked in shock, trying to piece together the details in his mind. Another shiver wracked his body, and he realized his covers had somehow fallen into a crumpled heap on the floor, leaving him in only a T-shirt, fleece pajama pants, and bare feet. He snatched the blankets and flannel sheet from the floor and pulled them up to his chin. He tucked the corners beneath himself, wrapping himself like a cocoon to settle his chattering teeth.

He took a deep breath to calm his nerves and forced himself to lie back down on the bed and relax. It was only a bad dream. He tossed and turned for long minutes, willing himself to forget, yet the flood of adrenaline continued to pump through his veins with vigor, making sleep elude him.

"Oh, forget it," Casey muttered, and tossed back the covers to climb out of bed. He flicked on the light switch to illuminate the room, then dug through his pile of clothes to find a hoodie and a thick pair of socks. He knew it would take a while to fall back asleep, so he might as well alleviate his mind in the process. Opening his toolbox of acrylic paints, he took out a small cup and went to the bathroom to fill it halfway with water. Then he dabbed his largest brush in Windsor blue and a little water to create a midnight blue wash across the top two-thirds of the canvas.

He used deliberate, brash vertical strokes of green and yellow mixed with a bit of titanium white to paint ribbons of colors dancing across the midnight sky. Careful to keep the abrasions on his palms clean, he washed out his brushes with his fingertips to cleanse them of any hint of green, then used lots of white with a little bit of cerulean blue and a light shade of violet in thick, truncated brush strokes across the bottom third of the canvas. The pale colors resembled puzzle pieces of glacial ice. While he painted, the sound of broken glassware rang in his ears, reminding him of the ice's unexpected strength to break through the glassy panes of the boathouse.

Satisfied with his latest work, he stepped back to view it in its entirety. Casey sighed, studying the first personal memory he had of his father. It may not have been a great memory, but it was his own.

Casey reflected on the unprovoked anger that had led his father to create the destructive ice heave. He knew deep inside that was different and refused to let this knowledge destroy his life like it had done to Hugh. Casey didn't expect he was capable of that type of aggressive force, threatening the lives and property of the fishermen in the icehouses, but then again, he had never had so much bottled anger expelled in a single moment. He remembered Taylor claimed he had shot the water fountain in her face when he stood behind her in line, and Owen claimed he had accidentally started a fire when fury consumed him. Still, those events seemed minor in comparison to the costly devastation his father had caused out on the lake.

A part of him wondered what other capabilities he would discover he possessed once he began to explore his element in depth. He also contemplated what kind of incredible tricks his grandmother had up her sleeve, hoping she might be able to teach him a few the next time their paths crossed. He'd give her some time to practice, of course, but he still had to hold up his end of the bargain…which meant he had a promise to keep.

CHAPTER SIXTEEN

Casey emerged from the pool, his chest heaving from exertion. His heart pounded loudly against his ribcage, making his pulse thud loudly in his ears and override the din of the cheering crowd. Water dripped down his chest and arms as he tore off his cap and goggles and ran his fingers through his hair to get a good look at his time. He finished only four-tenths of a second shy of his personal best.

Casey sighed. After completing his last Sections race and qualifying for States in all three of his individual events, an uncomfortable hollowness filled his gut. He looked at the team bench and caught a glimpse of the creases of disappointment written across his coach's face. It seemed nothing short of setting a new record pleased Coach Harris these days. Sure, Casey's times were a bit off—even he expected himself to finish faster. But he still had plenty of opportunities to improve. Maybe Coach Harris simply had set really high expectations—perhaps impossibly high, especially with everything Casey had going on in his head these past few weeks.

He walked over to join his team, bracing himself for the

imminent lecture.

Coach Harris met him halfway to the bench. "Casey," he said, "I know you haven't finished your taper. But you've got to get it together, or States will be much tougher than you expect."

"Yes, Coach," Casey replied automatically. He knew this was not the time for excuses. His gaze fell to his feet, watching a small pool of dripping water collect around his toes.

Coach Harris placed a firm hand on Casey's shoulder, encouraging him to raise his head and look him straight in the eye. Beneath the initial disappointment, he detected understanding and compassion and allowed himself a small breath of relief.

"Casey, you know it's my job to push you farther than you imagined and make sure you're prepared to reach your goals in this sport. It's not an easy job, but it's definitely worth it. I have every faith that you'll do what it takes to achieve your dreams." He graced Casey with a rare smile, then walked back to rejoin the rest of the team.

Casey forced a small grin in return, but on the inside, felt overwhelmed with a sudden wave of sadness. Coach Harris's unexpected honesty acted like a kick in the pants, getting his mind back on track to finish what he started. He wouldn't make it to the Olympic Trials unless he pushed himself beyond any of his previous accomplishments. All of those accolades he'd received were in the past; it was time to move on.

Still, a small part of him wondered if that lofty goal mattered anymore. Did he even care about racing the best athletes across the nation? Or better yet, from around the world, should he even make it to the Olympics?

He felt a sharp nudge in the elbow. He turned, surprised to find Owen Teague standing next to him, drying his shaggy red hair with a beach towel. "How's it going?"

Casey shrugged. "I've been better," he admitted.

"From the looks of it, you did pretty decent today. Made States in all three of your events. Not bad. I'm surprised your fan club isn't here to congratulate you," Owen teased, giving him a soft punch in the shoulder.

Casey scratched his head. "I have a fan club?"

He grinned widely. "You know...that cute reporter from the school paper."

"Oh, Mandi? Nah. I think she pretty much hates me."

"Really? Why's that?" Owen asked, his grin fading.

Casey sighed. "I guess I blew her off in bio after getting next to no sleep from thinking about ellies."

"Seriously?" Owen did a poor job of covering his laughter with this hand. "You actually had elly *nightmares*?"

"Shut up. They weren't nightmares," Casey grunted, shoving the thoughts of crimson currents, sunken ships, and giant waves of ice to the back of his mind. "Besides, you're not making me feel any better."

"Actually, that's why I came to find you. I think there's someone here that might help."

"I seriously doubt that," Casey replied.

He jabbed his thumb toward the door. "Meet me outside the locker room after the meet, and I'll show you."

"Okay," Casey agreed in a disheartened tone. "Whatever." No one could improve his mood at the moment. The only thing that would help was to clear his head and get it together by States. Now, all he needed was a plan.

Casey sighed again. Too bad he was completely out of ideas.

* * * *

After cleaning up, Casey texted his mom to tell her he needed a few minutes to catch up with Owen before heading home.

Not a problem, she texted back. *I have papers to grade.*

Big surprise there, Casey thought; she always had papers to grade and usually carried them with her in a large purse-like bag in case she had a few minutes of downtime between his events.

He exited the locker room and instantly spotted a faint citrus steam hovering over Owen's damp hair as he leaned against the brick wall of the hallway, deep in conversation with a girl with long dark hair framing her round face and olive skin. Before Casey could wonder if she was the person Owen wanted him to meet, her dark eyes turned, staring straight at him.

He didn't recognize her, but she seemed to know exactly who he was.

Owen waved him over. Casey approached with reservation, still uncertain as to how meeting this stranger would improve his attitude about anything, particularly swimming.

"Casey, this is Flora Fernandez."

"Hi," he said in a meek voice and politely stuck out his hand to greet her, trying to remember why her name rang with familiarity.

"She's the tennis player I told you about," Owen continued in an attempt to help Casey jog his memory.

Casey barely listened to Owen's explanation. His hand tingled at her touch, like a layer of cooled air swirled against his palm, bridging the gap between his skin and hers. He stared at his hand with surprise, then looked up at Flora. Her long dark hair lifted off her shoulders and whisked backward. Probably from the breeze from the open door down the hall, Casey assumed.

Owen's eyes widened at their exchange. "Not here, you two. There's a secluded spot over by the cafeteria. Why don't we head over there instead?" he suggested. He wrapped his arms around both of their shoulders, breaking their handshake, and directed them away from the crowd of swimmers leaving the locker room.

"What was that about?" Casey whispered to Owen once they had passed earshot of others leaving the meet.

"Well, Señor Observant, in case you hadn't noticed, Flora is one of us."

She turned to Casey, a soft smile settling across her face.

Casey's mouth fell open. "That thing with your hair...it wasn't the wind rushing in through the open door?"

Owen smacked himself in the forehead with dismay. "I'm sorry, Flora. Sometimes people say swimmers have too much chlorine on the brain."

"Ohhh," Casey glanced over his shoulder, just to make sure no one else could hear their conversation, before dropping his voice to a whisper, "she's the air elly All-American you told me about."

Flora's mocha colored eyes twinkled, obviously pleased with Owen's description. "Owen told me you were having trouble coming to grips with this whole thing, so he wondered if I could help you out," she explained.

"If you're a tennis player and an air elemental, isn't that considered cheating?" Casey dared to ask.

"I don't think so because I don't consciously think about my moves. It's not like I snap my fingers, and the ball magically stays in on my return. I still have to practice all the time and devote my life to the sport. I've made tons of sacrifices, just like anyone would have to who wants to become the best. Most of the time, I don't even think about it. I simply play my game," Flora added. "But when I'm really concentrating on a serve, I'll sometimes feel the wind pick up behind me. It's not like I'm asking it to help me out. It just sort of does. Like it gives me a little more power behind my serve or propels me with that last little burst to reach a ball. Things like that, I suppose."

"But how do you actually know you're an air elemental?" Casey countered. "What I mean is, how do you know it's actually your powers? Maybe you're really not any different than everyone else. Maybe your talent and hard work was all that got you this far."

"This is how." Flora pulled her phone out of her pocket and scrolled through her photos until she found just the right one. After rotating her screen for Casey to see, she pressed "play" with her thumb. "If anyone ever asks, I tell them I was working on a project for my multimedia class, and it was a really windy day."

Casey watched the video of her striding barefoot beneath the warm summer sun, right through the middle of a field filled with blooming dandelions. Each step kicked up a white cloud of dandelion seedlings. Her hands left her side, her palms facing downward. The seedlings took to the air, drifting in a dancing current of white in her wake.

She spun toward the camera and flashed a knowing grin, then tightly closed her eyes. Her brow furrowed in concentration before she lifted her hands toward the sky. The white wispy seedlings rose, encircling her body. On the audio, Casey heard the wind's whistle carry across the field, responding to her whim. Each seed launched to new heights, riding Flora's breeze on personalized miniature parachutes as if she commanded the plants to perform a silent, synchronized choreography.

Casey stared at her image through the swirling white cloud of seedlings, convinced only an air elly could perform such a magical feat. He noticed one patch of dandelions off in the corner of the screen had remained perfectly still throughout the entire shoot, an impossibility if the wind itself had naturally created this amazing spectacle. He expected all of the dandelions would have responded to its whim.

On the screen, Casey watched Flora open her dark eyes and let her hands slowly drop back to her sides. The wind tapered, and the seedlings floated softly to the ground, coating the field in a fluffy layer, like a fresh coat during winter's first snowfall.

"Well?" she asked as the video concluded with the last few dandelion seedlings settling to the ground behind her. "Still think it's only raw talent?" She turned off her phone and slipped it into her pocket.

Awestruck, Casey shook his head. "Definitely not. But how

do you keep it hidden? Aren't there times when your opponents grow suspicious?"

She gave her head a small shake. Her long hair suspended for the slightest of seconds with each toss of her head. Casey likely wouldn't have noticed if he didn't know to look for it.

"Have you ever used your powers in any other sports?" Casey wondered.

"Yeah," Flora said with a small chuckle. "Golf. But I was so bad at driving the ball that I instinctively called upon the wind to help me out. It was way too obvious. With my poor form, there was no way I should've been able to drop the ball onto the green at every hole. So I decided to stick with tennis instead. I don't think of it as cheating since I don't intentionally call upon the wind. But I have noticed that other air ellies like me tend to gravitate toward sports like tennis, golf, archery, and volleyball."

"Just like water ellies are drawn to swimming and water sports," Casey noted.

"Exactly. But every now and then, you get someone who breaks the mold and finds an innovative and unexpected way to use his or her powers for success," she added.

"Like Owen." Casey thought back to his first race against Owen, back to the time when he didn't even know elementals existed. Casey had instantly noticed everything seemed different about him: his startling speed, the color of the water as his hand sliced through the surface in rapid strokes, even the temperature of the pool was distinctly warmer near his lane. He could hardly believe how much his life and his perceptions had changed since then.

"Yeah. Owen definitely breaks the mold." She gave a hearty laugh.

"Are you talking about me?" Owen asked, his voice filled with mock irritation.

"Sure are," Flora responded.

"Well, I hope it's all good."

"Some of it is and some of it…not so much," she teased. For once, Casey noticed, Owen didn't have a retort.

* * * *

The entire ride home, the video of Flora in the field of dandelions replayed in Casey's mind. Only one reason existed to explain how the swirl of dandelion seedlings carried high into the air on a perfectly still day. Sure, she could have lied to him and secretly been a whiz at videography, but nothing about her mannerisms suggested deceit. Plus, Casey might have questioned her work if he hadn't noticed that solitary patch of dandelions standing perfectly still in the edge of the frame.

Once he unpacked and got a bite to eat, Casey headed straight to his room and grabbed a fresh canvas and his toolbox of paints. When inspiration struck, he knew he had to act or else he'd lose the feeling entirely like he had with the deep-sea nightmare at his grandma's house. The pencil sketch hadn't held enough emotion to transfer his feelings into color days later. He knew he must paint his vision now, or it would never seem the same.

He selected tubes of cerulean blue and titanium white to mix together with water. Using long, even strokes, he created a background wash of light blue streaked with white for the occasional wispy cloud in the midday sky. Casey intentionally left the paint thinner than normal, knowing he had to work fast to achieve the effect he sought in this next stage.

Mixing white and cadmium yellow next, he touched the tip of the brush to his wet canvas. Each dot of light yellow paint spidered outward, resembling the top of the seeds' parachutes to capture the wind and spread the seeds to new areas. A swirling vortex of air caught each seedling. They took to the sky and spiraled upward in flight.

Casey painted the seeds larger in the foreground, then progressively smaller as they trailed higher and higher into the air, resembling tiny specks at the top of his piece. With a quick flick of his smallest brush, he attached a downward facing stem to each parachute, angling them with their neighbors as they rode the invisible breeze. In the corner, a solitary patch of cotton balls sat high on pink stalks, more closely resembling a creation from a Dr. Seuss children's story than actual plants.

Once finished, he set down his brush to study his work and grimaced, even though this wasn't the first time another girl elly had inspired one of his paintings. Luckily, that fact didn't look at all apparent to anyone but himself. From this distance, the light yellow seedlings almost resembled miniature amorphous amoebas from his pond water lab in biology class. Decked in waders, Casey and his classmates had observed aquatic wildlife and collected samples of pond water to bring back to the classroom and observe the single-celled organisms under the microscopes. Except that amoebas didn't have sticks attached to their bodies like the seedlings in his painting.

Still, no one should be able to tell he had intended his painting to capture the dandelions from Flora's video. No one but Casey…and he'd like to keep it that way.

CHAPTER SEVENTEEN

At States, Casey knew what to expect the moment he entered the pool for the individual medley. The familiar aroma of chocolate chip cookies fresh out of the oven overpowered the chlorinated air as he dove off the blocks. The colors and heat exuding from Owen in the adjacent lane no longer surprised him. This time, he used it to his advantage, pulling ahead of Owen on the butterfly to assure he could match his competitor's pace on the two lengths of backstroke that followed. His freshly-shaved arms and legs tingled against the water as he sliced through the swirling shades of teal green and aquamarine blue, marking his path where he encountered less resistance in his lane. His limbs felt glossy smooth, and streamlined as a flurry of mint green and pale yellow bubbles zoomed across his body, allowing himself to push his body faster than ever before.

On the breaststroke lengths, Casey took deep pulls with his arms and beat his legs into powerful whip kicks. During each breath, he peeked out of the corner of his eye at his competition but found his ability to sense Owen's presence underwater served as a better indicator of how he would fare against the Great

Plains' star. He held nothing back on the freestyle, slamming his palm into the wall with a huge splash. The finish was so close, he couldn't tell whether he or Owen won.

He raised his head above the water. His chest heaved from exhausting his last supplies of energy on his strong finish. "Nice race," he mustered between ragged breaths and congratulated Owen by knocking knuckles with his friend over the lane line.

"You, too," Owen wheezed, his voice haggard from the race.

The steam rising off his body appeared a deeper shade of orange-red than Casey had previously seen. He guessed Owen had expended more heat and energy than the last time they had raced in order to make his glow that pronounced.

It took Owen a few moments to catch his breath to string together the rest of his thoughts. "Wonder why they haven't posted the times yet?"

Casey stripped off his goggles and swim cap and stared at the blank scoreboard with rapt attention. Off to the side of the pool, he noticed several race officials engaged in deep conversation, like something seemed amiss.

He continued to bob in the pool, waiting with Owen for several minutes after the rest of their heat had touched the wall and exited the pool. Casey used the time to let his breathing return to normal. While he stretched his heavy arms and legs to help the lactic acid slowly depart his muscles, he pondered what issue had arisen to cause such a delay in posting the results. He tried to settle his nerves by replaying the entire race in his head until he convinced himself with absolute certainty that he had not made any stroke errors that could cause a disqualification from the event. Finally, the officials posted the finish times.

"Are you serious?" Owen exclaimed, slapping both of his palms against the surface of the water with a huge splash. He dove over the floating lane line and locked one arm around Casey's neck in a jubilant hug.

His arm felt expectedly hot, like a blistering sunburn across Casey's neck, but he didn't shy away. Instead, he stared transfixed, one hand grasping the buoyant lane line for support, uncertain if what he thought he had seen was actually real or simply a figment of his imagination. Had he actually finished that fast? He blinked in disbelief.

Apparently, he had.

Not only had Casey and Owen each achieved their personal bests, they had actually tied…down to the one-one hundredth of a second. His mouth spread into a full, satisfied grin. "Yes!" he shouted, and pounded one fist on the water with enthusiasm, then turned to Owen and ruffled his steaming head of hair. He had finally accomplished his goal and had beaten the qualifying time requirement for the Olympic Trials! Better yet, he and Owen would compete together against the best swimmers in the nation in this event. An initial rivalry turned camaraderie had enabled them to push each other beyond any of their previous accomplishments and achieve his long-lasting dream.

He allowed himself a minute to enjoy the moment with Owen before climbing out of the pool, dripping onto the pool deck. Casey spotted Mandi Howe's recognizable head of bouncing curls as she wound her way through the gathering crowd of officials at the side of the pool.

"Your fan club's back," Owen joked, and gave him a fast jab in the ribs.

"Not exactly. She only came here to see you," Casey amended.

"Really?" Owen's eyebrows peaked with interest. He quickly ran his fingers through his damp hair. Casey noticed he also straightened his weary shoulders, standing a little taller before she arrived.

Mandi bounced up to their lanes carrying a small notebook and a pen in her hand. Casey wondered if she'd decided to go old school after the last time she got wet with the heightened activity by the side of the pool.

"That was absolutely amazing!" she exclaimed. "A tie! Ohmigod, who would've thought? I doubt that's ever happened before in the history of Westlake. Or the history of States, for all we know. And now maybe the Olympics...I bet we'll make the front page again with this story!" Her face glowed with infectious excitement. Casey couldn't help but smile in return.

She leaned toward him, her voice almost a whisper in his ear. "Any chance I can still get you to share how you can 'read the water'?"

Casey thought how his initial explanation of synesthesia now seemed infinitely better than the actual truth. He doubted many people even read her articles, always wrapped up in their phones at the end of class. Still, there wasn't a chance he'd admit the *real* reason now. His water elly abilities would have to remain a secret.

Casey shook his head. "Sorry."

Mandi's lips turned down into a pout. Casey thought her expression didn't suit her attractive face.

"Well, there's always next year," she said with a hopeful shrug.

"Yep," Casey automatically replied, waiting until she had walked back to the stands with a little less bounce in her step before adding, "Not a chance."

"You shouldn't be so hard on her," Owen scolded.

Casey was quick to retort, "You're only saying that 'cause she couldn't take her eyes off you."

Owen's reddish eyebrows arched high on his forehead. "And that's a bad thing?" he asked with a perfectly candid grin.

Casey snorted. "You can go ahead and dream. I've got other things to think about...like the Olympic Trials."

"Yeah, boy!" Owen slapped Casey's hand in a congratulatory fist bump.

The Olympic Trials. Casey let the words lie on his tongue.

After all he'd been through, he had actually done it. A flurry of memories buzzed through his head: the empty yellow boogie board drifting far out at sea, Uncle Jim sweeping Jason's limp form from his drained arms, the concern and surprise written across the faces of strangers amassing around him on the beach, and the alarmed look that passed over his mom's face at his mention of the red water warning of danger. He had never imagined those initial signs indicated anything beyond a medical condition.

His thoughts quickly shifted to the citrus glow surrounding Owen's body in the water, Lee's remarkable half-court shot casually lobbed behind his back, Taylor's delicate frozen butterflies carried on the breeze, Hugh's destructive and uncontrollable fury released in the ice heave, and Flora's video of dandelion seedlings streaming high into the air on invisible currents. These recent revelations of elemental powers had threatened to strip him of everything he once hoped to achieve.

And yet, he did it: he persevered through the unexpected challenges that stood in his way, just at the time when it had mattered most. His blue eyes sparkling in the overhead lights, he ran his fingers through his tangled wet hair, combing it away from his eyes. Water trickled down his smooth, shaved arms and pooled around his feet as he stood, staring in amazement at the results. He allowed himself a deep breath of relief before breaking his gaze to share his joy with the team.

Juggling his clipboard and stopwatch in one hand, Coach Harris shuffled across the slick pool deck, meeting him halfway to the bench. He held up his free hand for a jubilant high five. "Now that's what I'm talking about!"

Casey's mouth slid into a wide grin. For the first time since he had learned about his water elly abilities, he had finally, *finally*, pleased his coach with his performance.

CHAPTER EIGHTEEN

Casey turned on his favorite playlist, letting the music's energizing beat stick in his head and psyche him up for his races as he set out a few bags to pack. He double-checked his essentials: swimsuit, warm-ups, team jacket, extra swim caps in case his split, and his best pair of goggles. He also tossed in a backup pair of goggles that he hoped he didn't have to use. He dreaded being that kid who had theirs fill up with water upon entering the pool just because he hadn't gotten a good seal.

He heard a knock on his bedroom door. Casey turned down his music and said, "Come in."

His mom propped the door open and leaned on the doorframe. "I just checked in for our flight and printed the boarding passes. Are you all set to go?" she asked with a poor attempt at containing the brimming excitement in her voice.

Casey nodded. "I'm almost done packing." His heart filled with the most confidence he'd felt in weeks. He zipped his backpack closed, satisfied he hadn't forgotten anything critical for the race.

"And your hair," she noted, pointing at the tangled auburn

mane that flopped over his eyes.

"Oh. Right." Casey wistfully ran his fingers through his hair he'd grown out all season...perhaps for the last time.

His mom's gaze fell on the growing stack of paintings in one corner of the room. "Y'know, I wanted to apologize to you. All this time, I simply thought you liked to paint abstract art. Grandma Louise told me. I'm sorry I didn't realize."

Casey suddenly felt his stomach flip upside down. "What did she tell you?" he asked, his expression frozen with fear.

"To appreciate your gift," she said with a small smile.

"My gift?" He scratched his head. Had Grandma Louise told her about his elemental powers? Or about hers? He shook his head at the impossible idea. He swore she had said it was a guarded secret.

"Your talent for art and swimming," Ellen explained. "She said your art wasn't abstract, but what you actually saw."

Casey gulped. He felt his heart begin racing so loudly he was convinced his mom could hear it in the awkward silence of the room. "She did?" he managed.

She gave a slow nod. "You've grown up so fast, I mean. I think Grandma Louise feels bad for some of her actions from the past, and she doesn't want me to make the same mistakes with you. I know you don't talk to me about it, but I'm sorry if I ever made you feel uncomfortable about how you view the water from your synesthesia."

A deep sigh of relief escaped his lips at hearing her last word. She still believed the doctor's diagnosis, meaning his grandma's water elemental explanation remained safe.

Ellen walked across the room and bent down to look at the stack of canvases in a pile on his carpet. "Do you mind?" she asked.

Casey shook his head, pushing the concern of the ice and air elly paintings to the back of his mind. The chance of her making those connections seemed extremely slim. "Go for it."

She flipped through the stack of canvases, pausing when she reached his painting of lime green and canary yellow circles in a variety of sizes.

"I know, I know. Bubbles are supposed to be white," Casey apologized.

"You really see them in this many different colors?" she asked. Her tone sounded more curious than fearful, unlike his first confession about the warning of crimson water at the beach.

"Every time. I know it's strange," he added, trying to justify his observations. "And I can't really explain why it happens, but—"

"No," she said, her eyes shining with admiration. "They're beautiful. Each one is so much more amazing than I ever realized. I wish I could see the world like you do."

Casey sighed. All this time, he'd spent trying to hide his differences instead of appreciating the gift he'd been granted.

"You know what I think?" she asked.

"What's that?"

"I think when we get back, it's time to redecorate the house."

Casey scrunched his nose. "Redecorate?"

"These don't belong in a pile on your floor anymore," she clarified. "I think you should show off your talent. We can hang them around the house."

"I dunno, Mom. It's kind of embarrassing," he said, his gaze automatically finding his feet. What if someone came over? His hobby wasn't exactly what people might expect.

"Oh, you don't have to tell anyone they're yours. We can arrange them however you'd like."

"Well, okay, I guess," he finally consented. "Except for these ones." He selected his favorite canvas right on top of the Carolina rip current and the yellow boogie board floating out to sea, along with his recent fire, ice, and air paintings stored at the bottom of the pile. "I'd like to keep these up here in my room."

He made a mental note to watch Mason Brown on the track this spring. He needed some inspiration to finish the missing piece in his gallery of other ellies like him.

"Sounds good." She wrapped her arms around Casey in a proud hug, then took a step back to tousle his hair. "Now, about that haircut."

* * * *

Casey set down the clippers and looked in the mirror, studying his unfamiliar reflection. A mass of auburn locks filled the sink basin, signaling the final stage in his preparation. He already missed his old hairstyle but guessed this new look would better suit him for the race. He'd cut his hair to a short coat of stubble on the sides and back but intentionally left about an inch of length on top. He liked how it tended to spike upward when he ran his fingers across his forehead. Although he expected some of his competitors to shave their heads completely bald, Casey feared a shiny dome would draw too much unnecessary attention to his protruding ears, so he'd prefer to stick with his trusty swim cap instead. With his new haircut, the cap should fit skin tight against his scalp.

Like other swimmers, he planned to shave down to reduce drag before his race, but that would have to wait until the night before the race. Though Casey had never grown accustomed to the naked feeling of having shaved arms — or the tiny prickly hairs as it started to grow back—he had to agree with his teammates that bare legs and armpits felt the weirdest of all. Still, he knew the results would prove worthwhile. Every time he had shaved in the past, he managed to drop his time by at least a second or more. He didn't intend to break that streak now.

"So, I guess that's it," he said aloud, taking one final look at his new reflection before cleaning the mound of hair clippings in the sink and sweeping up the strands strewn across the floor. Physically, his body felt taut and well rested. His muscles had grown antsy from the taper, a sure sign he'd be ready to explode off the starting block. He only hoped his mental state would hold together now that he had closure. It was a gift…a gift he willingly chose to use without reservation. A gift he deserved.

Casey's phone buzzed in his pocket, interrupting his thoughts with an alert of a new text message. He set down the dustpan and slid his finger across the screen, surprised to see Taylor Sperry's name pop up.

Wanted to ask you…do U want to catch a movie tonight?

A movie? Under any other circumstances, that sounded like fun. He figured she had gotten a bunch of friends together and thought she'd invite him to take his mind off his upcoming meet. He quickly texted back.

Can I take a rain check? I'm leaving first thing in the morning.

He sent the message, hoping his plan to get to bed early wouldn't sound like a lame excuse for letting her down. Would she even bother to ask him again in the future?

Another water e joke? At least this time U have a good excuse.

Casey smiled, noticing she still used the "e" in place of "elly."

Sorry.

No problem. But promise me one thing.

What's that?

Kick some butt at the Trials!

You got it.

Good luck!

She added four emoji four-leafed clovers, and a smiley face after her last message.

Casey set down his phone and flopped back onto his bed. He ran his fingers across the stubble on his head. It prickled and felt foreign to his touch, reminding him of the reason why he had given himself a buzz cut. He knew there were so many other things he should be thinking about to prepare for his last event of the season, and yet….

Taylor Sperry. He envisioned her long black ponytail

swishing back and forth over her jersey number as she had carried the puck around a defender before passing it to her teammate on a give-and-go, her stick poised and ready on the crease for the return pass with a quick wrist shot to score a goal. He thought of the rage that had consumed her face when she first saw him at the rink after her game and the anger lacing her voice when she claimed she had intentionally switched schools to avoid spending another minute with him. And he remembered her graceful icy butterfly that had swooped overhead before alighting on the tip of his nose.

After Taylor's hostile initial reaction toward him, who would've ever thought she would grow to like him? Especially after all the pain he had unintentionally caused her in elementary school. He still felt really bad about accidentally dumping blue paint on her white Wild jersey, but to be honest, he couldn't remember the episode at the drinking fountain at all. Could it be that he'd spent the whole time waiting in line for the drinking fountain thinking of other things, like how to block out the deafening gurgling of the water or trying to understand why he tasted apple pie with whipped cream when nothing on his lunch tray even came close to resembling that dessert? Casey figured if it had made her that mad, he was quite positive it must have actually happened. At least she hadn't brought up the other half dozen events on the Spring Hill playground that had also infuriated her during their elementary years.

Still, she had wished him good luck. Casey suddenly felt his heart flutter at the thought of seeing her again. He knew he should drive his emotions to the back of his mind, but he still had some time before he needed to turn off his lights. He ran his fingers over his short head of hair, still not accustomed to its length, and let himself lie in bed for a few more minutes, dreaming about the possibilities.

EPILOGUE

"We're so proud of you, Casey," Aunt Samantha beamed, and pulled him into a quick hug. "I can't believe you're here and that we'll get to see you race in person." She released her nephew, her gaze shifting between Casey and Ellen. "It's really nice to see you all again."

"You deserve this," Uncle Jim said and gave his hand a firm shake in congratulations.

"Thank you," Casey replied, glancing in particular at his cousin Jason with a wide smile. "I'm really glad you could all make it."

When he qualified for the Olympic Trials in Raleigh, North Carolina, Ellen called her sister to see if they might have time to come and watch his race. He had never really expected they would all make it. Years had passed since the last time he had been able to visit his cousin on the East Coast. And on that occasion, Aunt Samantha and Uncle Jim intentionally made sure to find lots of activities to entertain Casey and Ellen that did not involve a trip to the beach.

Ellen quickly wrapped her arms around him for good luck.

"You should probably get ready," she suggested with a wave of her hand. "You'll have plenty of time to catch up with everyone afterward."

Casey nodded. "Thanks again for coming," he told them, his confidence buoyed inside his chest, knowing others had come here to support his accomplishment.

Ellen headed toward the stands with Aunt Samantha and Uncle Jim, but Jason purposefully lagged behind. He glanced over each shoulder, then nervously ran his fingers through his waves of sandy blond hair. Jason swallowed hard before speaking.

"I should've told you this a long time ago. I just couldn't get the words to come out right. See, I couldn't talk about the accident for a long time. I hate to admit it, but I had nightmares about the ocean for years afterwards. I don't know if I ever told you this face to face, but I wanted to thank you for saving my life that day at the beach. I don't know how you got us out of that rip current, but you did. And y'know, if you were able to accomplish something like that when you were just a kid, I can only imagine what you'll be able to do today. I know you'll be great." He held up a fist to bump against Casey's.

Casey beamed, his heart swelling with pride to receive such high praise from the cousin he had idolized throughout his childhood years. He could hardly believe that Jason would soon graduate and head off to college in the fall, or that in just two short years, Casey would find himself in that very same situation.

After waving goodbye to Jason, Casey walked over to the team bench to set his bag down. A few minutes later, the meet officially began with the National Anthem. Casey took off his hat and placed his hand over his heart. During the song, he peeked over to the stands to gauge his mom's reaction and caught her wiping a tear from her eye. Whether from pride of seeing her son race at this level or from her worry that he was growing up too fast, he couldn't be sure.

Just then, at the time when the music reached the "rocket's

red glare," a man entered the upper seating area dressed in a thick flannel shirt, jeans, and a trucker style baseball cap. Casey's heart skipped a beat when he recognized the man's unsteady gait.

"No way," he breathed.

Unaccustomed to the humidity and heat inside the warm pool area, the man quickly unbuttoned his flannel shirt and shed his outer layer to reveal a T-shirt with a massive fishhook on the front, impossible to miss even from his distance. As the song concluded with a drawn out "home of the brave," the man ambled down the bleachers, purposefully stopping next to Ellen Donnelly. Casey watched in utter disbelief, his hand frozen over his heart, as the man turned to face her, his mouth forming words.

Ellen's jaw dropped. Even from this distance, Casey could detect the surprise registering across her face. Her lips seemed to say, "Hugh? Is that you?"

While the other swimmers had returned to their seats on the bench, Casey remained standing while his hand slowly fell to his side, long after the song's last note. He knew his father's actions had caused her incredible hurt. Casey wondered if maybe she would realize that although Hugh couldn't repair his relationship with her, he wanted to be there to support Casey.

From Casey's vantage point, he couldn't make out Hugh's face. Yet the defeated slump in his shoulders appeared to respond with something that looked a whole lot like, "I'm sorry."

Judging by Ellen's expression, she had accepted a portion of his apology. Aunt Samantha, Jason, and Uncle Jim politely slid down the bench, making room for Hugh to join them. Casey never expected a full reconciliation from either of them, but he had to admit, this was a start.

Owen interrupted his thoughts with a quick nudge to his elbow. "You planning on standing like a statue all day? If so, it'll make my job a whole lot easier."

"Huh?" Casey asked.

"The song ended like a minute and a half ago," Owen noted with a laugh.

"Oh," Casey said and belatedly took a seat, feeling the blood rise high in his cheeks. His gaze shifted to his friend, and he noticed Owen had decided to go the bald route to prepare for the race.

"It's all gone," Casey said with a soft whistle of amazement. He ran his hand over his friend's shiny head, accustomed to seeing it smothered with a mess of flaming red hair. The smooth, shaved skin felt exceptionally warm beneath Casey's palm. "I think I can see my reflection," he teased.

"Very funny," Owen said in a flat voice. "I'd never done it before, so I figured, hey, why not?"

"So, how do you like it?" Casey wondered.

"I hate it," Owen admitted. "But if it helps me beat you, then it's worth it," he said with a widening smirk.

"Touché." Casey laughed and began his familiar routine of stretching out his arms and legs.

"Let's go. We're up soon," Owen said with a nod toward the starting blocks.

Casey couldn't believe it. All the time and preparation leading up to this moment, all the agonizing practices and pushing his body to new limits, all the sacrifices he'd made, and all the challenges he'd overcome. This was it. Casey grabbed his cap and goggles and took a deep breath, trying to keep his mind from reeling. He didn't dare let any other thoughts overwhelm him at this final stage in his swimming season.

The race announcer started the heat before them. Casey's stomach tensed as he watched the swimmers take off at a phenomenal speed. He blinked in awe, never witnessing this intense level of competition before.

"Hey, check that out," Owen said, nodding toward the swimmer preparing for their heat in lane two. "Can you say, hashtag elitist snob?"

"Why's that?" Casey asked, turning his head.

Owen pointed to the swimmer's left leg. He wore a small tattoo depicting four wavy lines in black just above his anklebone. Each line resembled the tilde over the "n" in Spanish, changing the pronunciation from "en-eh" to "en-yeh" or two wavy equal signs signifying "approximately equal to" in math class, one stacked directly above the other.

"Stuck up, purist," Owen sneered.

"What are you talking about?" Casey wondered, finding Owen's tangent difficult to follow as usual.

Owen rolled his eyes. "Some ellies think they're better than others."

One eyebrow perched high on Casey's forehead. "How so?"

Owen leaned toward Casey and whispered his reply. "They believe the original documented four elements are the only ones who deserve elly abilities. Earth, air, fire, and water. That's it."

"Really? What about ice?" Casey asked. His mind instantly drifted to Taylor.

"My point exactly," Owen agreed.

"So you're saying this swimmer's also an elly? But I thought ellies wanted to keep their abilities a secret," Casey said in a low voice so only Owen could hear.

"Yeah, they do. But some like to flaunt their powers. If anyone asked, he would tell them the design merely represents the four elements, nothing more."

"Maybe you're just reading between the lines," Casey noted, remembering his grandma's history book. The story had changed dramatically when she told him additional information that never made it to print. "Besides, what kind of elly do you think he is?"

"Most likely water, though he'd probably cover it up if you asked him directly. Luckily, there are other ways to tell."

Casey nodded. Owen's ability to spot another elemental had opened his eyes in ways he never imagined possible since the first time they met. With another elly in their heat, Casey expected this race to challenge him unlike any other.

"Then let's give him a race he'll never forget," Casey suggested.

"You got it." Owen held up his knuckles to knock against Casey's fist. "Good luck."

"You, too," Casey said with a widening grin. Though he knew this wouldn't be easy, the heat he felt from Owen's fist bump served as a reminder of the common bond they shared. Casey found it funny how his perceptions had dramatically changed since their first encounter in the one hundred backstroke only a few weeks ago. He had originally perceived Owen Teague's startling heat as a threat. Now the knowledge of others like him fueled his reserves, providing him with support and encouragement from the secretive community of ellies.

Casey's eyes drifted to the bleachers surrounding the poolside. He spotted recruiters in the stands wearing hats and polo shirts from prestigious college swim and dive programs across the nation. He recognized the collegiate symbols for Yale, Duke, Dartmouth, and Johns Hopkins, to name a few. The results from today's competition completely mattered. He knew they did.

Casey bent down by the side of the pool and filled his cap with water. He held the brimming swim cap overhead and doused his hair. It took practically no time to tuck every bit of his short hair into place. He shook out his arms and jumped up and down exactly three times to loosen his legs. Casey adjusted his goggles into place and gazed at the scoreboard, cementing his goal in his mind.

On the official's signal, he stepped up onto the blocks with the other swimmers from his heat. A flurry of thoughts sped through his mind. He had already qualified for this meet as a high school sophomore, while he guessed most of the swimmers here were in college or even older. He had plenty of time for future growth. He glanced at his mom and dad engaged in conversation in the stands. They had a long way to go, but it was a start. And the rain check from Taylor. He hoped she'd take him up on that movie once he got back home.

Casey refocused his attention on the race. Grandma Louise's words echoed in his head, *Give it all you've got. Hold nothing back. Then regardless of your results, you will be a winner.*

"Swimmers, take your marks," the official announced.

"No regrets," he reminded himself and bent over to wrap his fingers firmly around the starting block. His flexed core and taught leg muscles stood poised, ready to spring into action.

At the sound of the buzzer, the crowd's cheers rose to a deafening roar, and Casey flew off the blocks, planning to follow every word of his grandmother's advice. His goal fixed in his mind, he soared through the air, piking in the middle of his dive, then entered the water. The noise of the crowd instantly muffled as a flurry of lime green and canary bubbles greeted him. Casey's skin tingled as the water streamlined over the exposed hair follicles of his freshly shaved body. The stimulated nerve endings felt like he had a mild version of an electric shock administered to his appendages, which heightened his state of alertness in an instant.

Casey snuck a quick glance out of the corner of his eye, surprised to see the water elly in lane two washed in a turquoise glow underwater. No wonder Owen recognized him instantly if that was how another water elly looked in his own element. Luckily, Casey already had a small lead on the elly in lane two, and he planned to keep it that way.

Focusing his attention back on his race, he aimed for the path of smooth blue-green colored water ahead. His rapid kick propelled him forward while his arms moved fast and free, unleashing energy in strong, powerful strokes. As Casey willed his body to go faster than ever before, a single thought filled his mind....

No regrets.

The End

After graduating from Cornell University with degrees in Biology and Education, Debbie Kump taught middle and high school science in Maui, Seattle, and the Twin Cities and worked as a marine naturalist aboard a whale watch and snorkel cruise. Debbie lives in Minnesota with her husband, two sons, and three Siberian huskies. She especially enjoys writing early each morning, teaching, coaching youth soccer, hockey, lacrosse, and baseball, and dogsledding her kids to school.

For more information, please visit her website: http://sites. google.com/site/debbiekumpbooks/